BEFORE
THE HOUSE
BURNS

This book is for
my parents and my sisters,
nowhere in these pages,
but whose goodness
I hope these pages honour.

BEFORE THE HOUSE BURNS

MARY O'DONOGHUE

THE LILLIPUT PRESS
DUBLIN

First published 2010 by
THE LILLIPUT PRESS
62–63 Sitric Road, Arbour Hill
Dublin 7, Ireland
www.lilliputpress.ie

ISBN 978 1 84351 1649

1 3 5 7 9 10 8 6 4 2

A CIP record for this title is available
from The British Library.

Set in 12 pt on 15.5 pt Centaur by Marsha Swan
Printed in Ireland by ColourBooks of Dublin

We used to call what ruined us the storm,
Though that suggests we could have seen it break
And barred the door.

—Clive James

It will be an island on strings
well out to sea and austere
bobbing as if at anchor.

—Maxine Kumin

His two-story house
he turned into a forest,
where both he and I are the hunters.

—Robert Bly

Little, I used to think that family *and* house *were one and the same thing. You had people under a roof, inside windows and walls. That was the big idea. That was how the world was planned and put together.*

If you lifted the roof on any one of them you'd catch the people like dolls. Stock-still in their various rooms, standing, sitting, their bent arms frozen in gestures or stirring something on the cooker. I never had a dolls' house, but a nearby girl, Ailbhe, did. She had me keep my eye to its dormer window for at least an hour one time. They'll come alive, *she said,* when they think we're not watching. They have a secret life, you know. *That was how I knew I could steal one of the occupants. I took the badliest dressed doll, the one with yellow hair and some of her toes chewed off. Ailbhe said the dog did it. But I bet she did. I knew the temptation. Once you first put the little paddle of a doll's foot in your mouth, it was hard not bite down on it. I jammed this doll in my dungaree pocket and from there into my schoolbag, and when Ailbhe came back I said that I hadn't seen them move and maybe they only did it at night-time. She never said anything to me about it, not a word about the doll's disappearance. And I never played with the doll, only stowed her under the beanbag in my bedroom.*

We lived on the lip of the city then, in a housing estate where red-tiled white houses stood in a horseshoe turned round a green. In the middle of the grass was a huge tree. Its branches spread low and wide, making a whispering green roof in summertime. In winter, grey clouds showed between and you had to slow your mind enough to focus on the fact that the clouds and not the branches were moving. A swing hung from one branch; it was there for as long as I'd known the tree and the green and the houses. Two lengths of thick blue-snake rope; two fat knots under a piece of timber. The timber was old-coloured like the branches: softish grey. Like it had been rained on thousands of times.

The houses stood guard around the green, a hundred or more windows looking out for all the children who played there.

The tree was the centre of the world.

And if you were on the swing, flinging up to the sky and biting down on the air that rushed at your face, then you were the queen of everything.

All the houses were separated by hedges. Some were in better shape than others, neat and squared off at the outside corners where they met the footpath. The messier ones had soft skinny twigs growing out; they stroked your face like gentle fingers when you went past. Some had big dips in the middle where a person or a bicycle or sometimes even a car had crushed into them.

All the doors were brown with wavery pale-green glass in a square window at the top. The glass looked like the backs of leaves. The letterboxes were stiff silver mouths that would snap your hand trapped if you weren't careful. Cats slunk to the back gardens through the narrow way between houses. There weren't that many cats. One house had a dog that frightened them and the children. I never saw it, only heard its rackety barks in a kennel out the back. It shouted like a tyrant. Don't. You dare. Come near me, *it seemed to yell. But I came to think that maybe it did want someone to free it from where it was boxed at the bottom corner of a garden. Its outrage started when I went to bed, and I became used to it. Enough to be able to fall into sleep, the bitter cries dwindling down as I slipped beyond them.*

Houses. I can remember leaving ours at the same time as other families left theirs a lot of mornings. Front doors crunked shut, then the doors of cars opened like big wings. Some people backed out onto the street, having preferred to park the nose of their car touching their front door. In those backers' cars you'd see the fathers' arms stretched along the passenger seats and their heads turned far round, vexed-looking as they worked to turn out onto the horseshoe street.

Years later I saw a film that showed a neighbourhood in America: identical houses, lawns, cars, people. The women had the same hairdos, big and bubbled around their heads; they walked out to collect their letters at the same time; they walked back to the door in time. At each door were two children, a boy and a girl, the boy older than the girl, chubby-cheeked and gleaming. Then the husbands came out, leaving for work and swinging the same lunchboxes from the ends of their crisp white-sleeved arms. Their ties looked knitted. I now know that it was meant to be making fun of the 1950s cardboard cut-out life, of the kind of thing everyone supposedly wanted. The big dream.

But knowing this doesn't impinge on the safety of the memory I'm sure I have, a memory of a time of things true and orderly. Being at the centre of a stripey blanket in the centre of the green. My father and mother sitting with their arms propping them from behind. Sitting this way made their arms look thin and hard, like gangly boys' arms. Lemonade spilled on the blanket, collecting in a pool instead of draining through. Biscuit crumbs behind my knees. Other families were there. Everyone drifted back to the houses when the evening arrived suddenly like a chilly surprise. People closed their doors and put on lights and television. The swing on the tree on the green was left to dangle alone for another night, and you knew without thinking too much about it that it had been a nice day.

Families were houses. The walls and roofs held people together. You lived inside; you played inside and around it, never too far away from it. When a family changed, often so did the house, either by having a new room built on, or a room turned into two, or a garage turned into a room.

When my sister came along, and later my brother, we didn't do any of those things.

Not long after my brother was born, all five of us were living in a house in another town. In a room in that house in that other town. There was a bathroom in the corridor and a correct time to use it; another family, connected to us by our mother, only we'd never met them before; two cats and a goldfish. It was only for a short time until things were supposed to come back to their right way. I think of it now as a collection of smells (cabbage, shoes, my baby brother's Milupa) and the voices of cousins we dreaded to hear coming up the stairs.

And I can't think of the word family without first considering the places that held us. And the secrets of our make-do life.

The house here now on this winter morning isn't before me at all, except as a big patch of blackened gum. You don't believe that buildings can burn to the ground, like the saying, until you can step over their tarry perimeter and walk on the innards.

The pile of car tyres my father kept inside the back door is gone, turned into bracelets of rusty wire. In more recent times he'd banked the tyres against the door to slow the progress of what he called 'marauders'. No-one would know up here in the hills if marauders came and killed me. Who would know. No-one. I used to imagine him lugging the tyres and piling them man-high and three wide. His arms and chest would smell of rubber, his hands would be blackened.

He sat across from me over a plate of lamb chops and mashed potatoes in the only restaurant he'd eat in: the dark pokey one in the oldest hotel in the town where we went each year for my birthday. He'd suck the last flitters of meat clinging to the lamb bone. Last year was my eighteenth and he talked about the age of reason, the drinking age, the age your brain starts to harden, the age by which some poets and composers were already past their best work. It was depressing and inspiring all at once. I had no grand artistic ambitions; I'd been drinking covertly since I was fourteen. I wasn't afraid of my brain hardening, as such, but maybe I'd prefer that it didn't solidify certain memories so as to make them the only things I woke and slept with.

It was a good birthday lunch, and he even smiled a couple of times, the old one belonging to photos. A smile like a rare relic.

The smell of the burned house rises chokey into my nose, like a cigar. Smoke that's still around, half a day later. As though the fire wants to prove to me how long it lasted. Fire is as greedy as anything; once it gains its first taste it won't let go without a fight. And there wouldn't have been a fight, for this house was on scrubby grass inside walls of trees, with no neighbours to notice a strange orange flicker outside their curtains. My father didn't have a telephone. He'd cut the line as soon as taking this place.

Then I heard the hens. He didn't get rid of them, like he threatened to do. Except I never believed him on that. They've all turned into clockers. Sitting and crying on eggs, the eejits. He told me that he'd learned how to whammle them from someone in town. Great word, whammle. Fantastic word. And so he put three hens into enclosed spaces, one under a crate, one into each of two compartments of an old dresser, until they learned to give up their hopes.

And now I could hear them crying in that shed at the end of the grass behind the house. I couldn't move to it, didn't want to open the door and unleash their shrieking fear into the morning air.

They had been awake while my father slept.

The garda who drove me here, slowly and silently along the narrow persecuting back roads, stands facing the car. His broad shoulders look cut from the flinty sky.

I know he turns to see what's going on when I run to the shed to shrug the tight bolt through. It seems to take an hour to free it. It gives up with a bitter yelp like fingernails on a chalkboard. The hens, who must've been batting themselves against the door until I arrived, are now shrinking in the corners. I hear their fluffed panic, smell their intimate stink. I scrabble the wall for a switch.

The shock of the sight sends me back a few steps. The hens are all perched on the huge dresser that takes up the back wall. Still and stunned and wide-eyed, they look like sculptures on an altar. They hold onto its shelves and edges like they'll never let go.

I run towards them shouting and they don't scatter until the last second, until I'm upon them, crying. I want to wring their necks for being alive and looking for attention while he is dead. All at once they disperse and move past me in a kind of stunted flight, like they don't know whether to take to the roof or the floor. Their feeble wingbeats release more of their close scent and I'm sure that I'll be sick.

Then I see that the dresser isn't mottled with henshit. Just like my father to clean it religiously and leave his own bath clogged with hair, his shaving mirror shadowy as a rain puddle. Just because it's an animal doesn't mean it has to live in confinement and squalor. *My father shouting at our neighbour who kept the dog with the big bark locked up. His fury comes to me suddenly, in one piece. I remember thinking that his words were the colour red that day. And I feel sure that he must've set that dog free one night.*

I move my hand across the dresser's greenish grain and imagine him wiping it yesterday or the day before. I pull on both drawers and they come out chock-full of bills and letters and clippings. I delve my hands into where his hands have been, I tousle through corners of paper that must've been smoothed by his fingers. He always hated flapped paper, corners turned down on library book pages or money.

A slim book at the back. I prise it loose. No; a notebook with a hard black cover. Covered in the sticky cellophane that we used to wrap our schoolbooks with for protection. Except I see that it's covered all the way round, bound in plastic with the closing edge cut neatly and pressed so tightly that it's hard to even make out the seam. I put it into my pocket. I know that I'll have to come back to clean out the rest. Or have someone do it. I could hire a man with a van to make the entire contents of this shed disappear in an hour.

But there's the problem of the hens. As I run out the door to try and gather them — cursing because I don't even know the headcount — I see the garda trying to corral them out near the car. I almost laugh: he's down low, nearly on his haunches, with his arms thrown wide. It's exactly what someone stopping cows on a road would do, except they'd be standing at full height. But he's very serious and hell-bent on not letting the battalion of hens pass.

Between us we manage to send two twaddling back to the shed and that done, the rest follow. I shut the door and make for the car.

There are things to do in the city, at the garda station. I have to do it, for I'm the eldest. I'm the one who got the phone call. I hope that the silent solid garda will come in with me.

There was no body found in the ruins getting smaller in the wing mirror.

But I could imagine a fire so ferocious that it might have turned him into a million black-paper iotas that flew away on the mountain breeze.

The telephone spoke of house and destroyed. I told them that I'd go there. They — that is, a woman with a Cork lift to her voice — seemed put out by my decision. Are you sure you don't want to send the guards on ahead of you? My snippiest voice told her, No, no, I want to see the house immediately. It felt like the first time I'd ever used the word immediately in a conversation. She said that she'd send a car to collect me.

From the five o'clock phone call to my long stunned face in the bathroom mirror to my two shaking hands on the tea mug, it didn't seem possible. I left the house without telling any of the nurses I shared it with what had happened. I walked to the car feeling like the last girl left on earth, being taken away in a garda car for her own protection.

But standing in the black mulch of the ruined house, among the powder of his dozens of books and jumble of clothes and the gee-gaws from markets and second-hand shops: that brought it all true.

There was no fight against this fire. It was powerful enough to heat the pine and perfume the woods like something that could anaesthetize you. The smell still spun in the morning air. It had leaped and danced and preened, and ate the little wooden house like a feast.

But what happens when the family burns before the house does?

Newmarket-on-Fergus, 1998

L. casei Immunitas

That's what's important this week. Since our father began the shopping list on Sunday night he's mentioned it at each mealtime. We won't be shopping until Friday. But he repeats its importance and takes out the list to put three stars beside what Maeve calls *the drinkie yoghurt*. His pencil is blunt and the stars are thickly scored, looking more like black explosions.

Bifidus Regularis. We need that. We need to be getting more of that into us. It's the latest fruit of his research. He sits back and slats his hands behind his head. *It's alive when it goes into you. A culture, as they call it. And then it makes sure that your insides are looked after.* I know that science will be my favourite subject at secondary school next year because I like thinking about the operations of things that work in anonymous armies inside us. In the case of my father's new friend *Bifidus Regularis* I imagine a sensation of friendliness and triumphant waving as it makes its way through his pipes.

We're at the kitchen table under a milk spill of light from the bare bulb.

Benny is under the table; it's his new place. Before this it was behind the long coat hanging in the back hall. You'd think a four-year-old would be a bit afraid of standing inside the heavy folds of a stranger's big coat. The abandoned coat, like the furniture and other things left around the house that's not ours, only rented, has its own smell. Something long-ago and lonesome. I suppose it belonged to the old man who'd died and whose daughter rented the place in a rush. You'd think Benny would at least find it unpleasant. But no, he'd stand there for as long as it took one of us to pretend we'd found him and snatch him out. Maeve had an idea that if we told him the truth of the coat — *a dead man's coat with his ghost inside its pockets* — he might give up hiding behind it. But there were things that Benny liked to do that it seemed unfair to stop him from doing. The way he liked to soften a biscuit in his mouth and then drop it into the palm of his hand and then lick it up again. Just because we found it creepy or disgusting didn't mean we should make him feel that way.

Benny had his techniques for handling things. He got used to this house much sooner than Maeve or I did. We'd go in the wrong doors, or misgauge the number of steps in the second flight of stairs after the turn, ending up a step short, tripping, feeling cheated by our own feet. Maybe a four-year-old moves through a place differently anyhow. Since they're smaller it's like they swim around it.

In the first week or so, I found Benny sitting on the armchair in the front room looking like a little king, one hand on each of the worn tapestry arms. Gazing out the window so steadily and deeply that my arrival didn't so much as produce a blink. I found myself suddenly frightened of whatever mysterious thing he was thinking. I sped over and lifted him out of the chair, a clumsy lift-cum-hug. He didn't appreciate it and kicked his way free. Then I saw that he was wearing a necklace. Pearls. I was ashamed that I didn't know if it was one of the house's lost things or something of our mother's. And so I couldn't rightly take it from him. He stomped off out the door, and I haven't seen the pearl necklace since.

While our father is detailing the benefits of *L. casei Immunitas* and *Bifidus Regularis*, reciting them like a list of features learned from a schoolbook, Maeve slides the shopping list toward herself and writes something on it. Probably something sweet. Or salty. Both together is the happiest time in her mouth: she loves to follow a crisp with a square of chocolate. My sister is eight. Last year she didn't make her First Holy Communion. It was during that time when we could've gotten away with anything we wanted, anything, and Maeve decided that she didn't want to eat something that the teacher said tasted like *sweet cardboard*. Nor did she want to wear a stiff white dress and veil. She didn't give in even when the teacher was reduced to telling her that she'd get a lot of money from people.

What people? Her face was as bold as ever I'd seen it, chin jutting out and cheeks superbly red. I was brought in to try and make sense to her. I stood next to the teacher feeling both a traitor to my sister and embarrassed at her resounding boldness. *Well, family people. Relatives. Friends of family.* Maeve said, *There are no such people, Miss.* That's when our father was brought into things. A phone call from school one evening. And that's when we knew we could get away with anything, for he clattered the phone down after saying, *If my daughter is opposed to this, then I don't intend to force her, and neither will I let you.*

Sometimes he spoke like another voice was coming through him. A voice from an old radio programme. Low and level and a bit snobby. Something set in motion by a button behind his ear: he always seemed to scratch there before the other voice began. It also happened at times when he was set on edge about something.

A squall in the vegetable shop about the price per pound on tomatoes. *Do you mean, sir, that I can't get these tomatoes for less at another seller?* The sir was a man he'd known for years. It was during that time when our father could've gotten away with anything, too.

Last week in the teashop when a woman said something about Benny. She thought she wasn't heard, but she had one of those loud old-person whispers. *Would you look at the state he brought the child out in.* Out in: it sounded strange. I concentrated on it to avoid my father winding up. The woman's tea companion tried to pretend she hadn't heard. *Will we take another cup, I'd know?* One of Benny's dungaree straps dangled for want of a button. For want of a button the horseshoe was lost. I could see what the woman saw: the slack and stained dungarees, the haircut our father had given Benny that morning. Benny had tough, thick, fair hair, the kind of hair it's fun to mess with and easy to twist into horns. It had been dampened from the kitchen tap for the cutting. Once cut and dried it sprang shorter than we'd anticipated. His blunt stunted fringe made him look like Friar Tuck.

Missus, I'll thank you to keep your opinions to yourself. Your opinion, should I say. I imagine that you have only the one. The tables were already close, so he didn't need to move in order to be heard. In fact, he didn't even turn his head to face her. But the way the woman looked at our father, alarm making her mouth open on half-chewed yellow cake, you'd think he'd pushed his face into hers like bad guys on television do when they're threatening people.

Poor Benny had gone under the table. He knew the trouble was about him. He had a fierce ability to gather embarrassment to himself and nurse it for all of us. He sat on our father's shoes and wouldn't come out until he'd seen the woman leave the teashop. When he did I could see that he'd tried to tug his fringe down, as Maeve had done that morning to stop our father from cursing at himself for being a *stupid bugger, useless bugger with a scissors.* She'd licked her fingers and applied them to Benny's hair, just like she was wetting a thread before sending it through the eye of a needle.

This gave a temporary improvement. And there was Benny, out from under the table with his fringe damp and spread flat to his skin.

D'ye think our small boy here would take some of that yoghurt with the Bifidus Regularis in it? Our father produces Benny from under the kitchen table like a magic trick. Benny curves into his arms like the baby of the koala bears Maeve still has in her room. *I think he'd do well on it.* Which worries me, for it reminds me of two months ago when he had all of us 'on' juice he made from crushed cabbage and spinach and a pile of other green things. He stewed it in batches in the biggest saucepan we had. The house smelled like something I remembered from a seaside trip: sewage coming from a pipe poking out of rocks. But it was good for us and it would prevent us from bad health. Being 'on' something meant eating or drinking rotten stuff to a schedule, lining up, no excuses. *Down the hatch, do you the world of good.*

Our father's getting more afraid of the world's random dangers every day. And more determined to make us immortal.

Maeve reads the list and thinks that her father should get one of the copybooks with the red and blue lines that teach Junior and Senior Infants how to write. Maybe it's the stubby pencil, but his letters are a stampede, then a chaotic collision at the bottom of the piece of paper where he ran out of space. She makes out *butter* and *milk* and thinks that these are the things that should be at the top of the list. The ordinary stuff that lives in fridges week in, week out. But he's got the *Bifidus Regularis* up there, and *fennel* (what?) and *mackerel*. Some time back she heard the weather announcer sounding very happy to tell everyone that they could enjoy a beautiful mackerel sky each evening for the next week. Her father sounded even more pleased to shout 'altocumulus' at the man standing as if propped by his elbow placed on County Clare.

Altocumulus. Wouldn't you at least use the proper term as well as the poetic one. Mackerel. Nothing like it, I always thought.

Maeve knew that she could learn a lot from her father, but it would be information that she would have to put into hibernation until she was older and it would be of use in some upper-level conversation or in a quiz like the one on television he watched all the time. *Final answer? Arragh, come on now, missus, are you that big of a dope that you don't know the capital of Colombia from your behind? Bogotá, for Jesus's* … He shouted at the people in the quiz chair like he shouted at the players in football matches. Maeve imagined that one day they might hear him and turn to look out and show him their middle fingers. Or, better still, come kicking out of the television like the soccer player who threw himself at someone who said something horrible in the crowd. Maeve remembered how he jumped feet-first with no thought about the fact that he too would fall down, and hard.

So every time she felt strongly about discovering an historical date or the name of a disease she worked to stash it like squirrels did with nuts. Coming back for them when they needed nourishment.

Now she's cross because there's no room left for her to write her items on the list, and if she keeps fiddling with it he'll notice and take it back. So she turns it and writes *marshmallows* along the side. Like a word that's climbing up the wall of the other words. She tries to make her writing look like his. But that's pointless, because her hand holds the memory of the teacher tightening her dry ringed hand around Maeve's when she went above the blue line for her small *a*s and *c*s and *e*s. That was three classes ago. The teacher, Miss Hyland, had a hand that was more like a hen's foot, red and rusky and with nails that looked like you would need garden secateurs to trim them.

Miss Hyland taught her how to write well and steadily, but she did so in a forceful way that Maeve was afraid she'd live with forever. Would her hand cramp up when she was writing a love letter to a boy? Would she sense Miss Hyland's dry chalky finger-pads pressing on her knuckles? For now, she only thought of it scientifically. She liked to play with boys – was one of the few girls in Third Class who still did – but there was none that she'd want to kiss.

Not like when she was five and she couldn't get enough of tasting Danny Connors's face. She'd made a complete show of him and herself when she'd sit down on the play-shelter bench and plant a smacker on his soft fat cheek. It was only ever Danny. Maybe because he looked a bit like a seal: he had no chin and his face seemed smaller higher on his neck than other people's. In the end Danny's sister had to ask Maeve's sister to sort it out. Laura Connors and Eva were in the same class. You wouldn't want to mess with Laura Connors, but it was easy enough to placate her. Eva said it to Maeve on the way home from school, shortly after she'd nabbed Danny in a headlock and kissed the top of his head. It was to be their last one. Eva wouldn't stand for any more of it; Laura Connors wanted it to stop: *It was totally embarrassing.* After the little speech was finished, Maeve began to recite, *My mother and your mother were hanging out the clothes,* and ran on ahead and threw loudly over her shoulder, *MY mother gave YOUR mother a PUNCH on the NOSE!*

Maeve imagined her sister and Laura Connors dressed in two aprons, pegging knickers on a line and then slapping each other on the shoulders and necks.

She knew what Laura and Danny's mother looked like: like she wasn't their mother at all, but some dainty little fairy woman who followed them around with permanently surprised eyes and trousers that billowed like parachutes in the wind and ended in tight cuffs at her ankles.

It didn't seem fair to put her own mother into the drama of the punch on the nose. And anyway the business was carried between Eva and the large motherly Laura Connors. When she ran in the back door panting and tasting acid because she hadn't wanted Eva to catch up with her, she collided with her father who grasped her by the shoulders and told her to take it handy. *What's all this sprinting for, hmm? Are we running from the hounds of hell today, is it?* She gulped in the soupy air of the kitchen. He was cooking with a host of saucepans again.

So kissing boys had ended and her handwriting had improved and she had behaved herself quite well for a good while.

The business about the First Communion still hadn't been fixed.

Maeve writes the word *pink* before the note on marshmallows. She has an idea for an experiment. She will melt the mallows and then mould them to her face in the shape of hideous scars. She will frighten Benny, and make Eva angry at her cleverness, by putting sticky ruckled skin all down one side of her face.

Under the table Benny studies everyone's shoes.

He himself is barefoot. What nobody knows is that today he reached up and dropped his shoes into the barrel under the drainpipe at the side of the house. He even tied them together so that they would drop to the bottom together. And live down there forever. He couldn't see the top of the water. But when he tossed the shoes in, some lapped out to thank him and ran black-green down the side of the barrel.

There is something about hiding things, burying them, mainly, that he likes the feeling of.

Eva has been looking for the necklace, he knows it, but she'll never find it. It's coiled in an empty shoe polish tin – he rescued it from the bin after seeing his father toss it there – and it's under the sand. Not the part of the sand pile that looks like a place to hide things; not toward the front. No. Benny went round the back of the sand as far as he could get before the briars hanging like hair over the wall clutched and stabbed him with their thorns. The sand on that dark side was damp and colder. Easy to dig because it came out in solid chunks, not like the powdery falling-back-in of a dig at the front. It stuck to his hands and he thought if he tasted it it would be like thick black salt. He put the tin in at a good depth and clotted the sand back around and over it. He thought about marking it. But there was no need. If he wanted to go back and dig it up he'd just look for the farthest spot he could get to under the briars.

That's where it would be. And Eva would never get to it.

He fixes on her shoes. They keep crossing and uncrossing. It's like she doesn't know whether to let the left one lead or the right one. This might be why she's no good at dancing, even though she practises in the kitchen with Maeve all the time. Benny thinks he never wants to learn dancing. His sisters seem so afraid of getting things wrong. Sometimes they include him. If they need to practise turning and going back to where they started. They tell him to stand still, *Don't move a muscle, Benny*, and they move around him and in and out through each other. One time they had him cross his arms so that he looked like he was hugging himself and they took a hand each and danced down to the back door, pulling Benny between them. Because they were laughing so much he started crying. It wasn't funny to pull him along like he was tied up. It gave him a scary feeling, like he'd fall any second and never be able to get up.

Eva's shoes are blue that used to be navy. He remembers how happy she was to get them. *Converse All Stars, Converse All Stars! Everyone at school wants these. Dadda how did you know?* The funny thing is, they make Eva's feet look longer and wider at the toes than her feet really are. Clown's feet, Benny thinks. But she loves them. He wonders what she would do if he took them to the barrel and sent them down to where his own shoes lay. Thinking about his shoes makes him shiver. It's night outside now. Benny is very afraid of night. It's when the boogie things come out. And his shoes are in more dangerous darkness than just night, for they're under all that dark water. He wants to get them back. Why did he do that?

Eva has drawn a tiny smiley face on each of the white caps on the toes of her shoes. They're so tiny that you might not see them at all if you were not as close as Benny is. Because the shoes were not new any more it was alright to do this, he supposed. Their father probably would not say anything if he noticed. Why did Eva draw these faces on her shoes? Maybe to make her smile when she saw them flashing back and forth when she walked.

Maeve is in sandals and socks. Sandals look strange with socks and the raggedy jeans she is wearing. The sole of one sandal is coming away and it gapes like the mouth of the plastic goldfish he brings to the bath. It looks like she could trip on it if she is not careful. Benny knows this because of the time their father spun forward and against the shelf of bread at the supermarket. He was ready to blame the floor until he saw that his shoe had burst at the front. When they all got back to the car, he pulled off his shoe and tore off the sole, the full sole, with his hands. It gave a nasty sound, lightly screaming as it came free. Benny wondered if to the shoe it felt like tearing a scab off. He knew what that was like: sharp burning, and then pain that fizzled down to pink. *Take that, you bugger,* said their father. Sounding like he had won something. But Benny could not understand being angry at the shoe and having to show it. For now he had an entirely broken shoe instead of one that he could have fixed with glue or nails or something from the drawer that held all the fixing things.

Maeve does not cross her feet like Eva. They simply sit there on the rung of the chair. Quiet and patient like cats on a wall. She must be busy doing something on the table.

His father's shoes are the new ones he bought from the table of shoes in the town. Benny was with him that afternoon; the girls were gone up to the shop that sold magazines and sweets. The man who sold them had a van full of shoes and boots behind the table. Benny could see in to where shoes and boots were piled high in the back corner. Their lace holes looked like thousands of eyes. Like the empty eyes of the dead jackdaw under the wall where the sheep came to scratch themselves. He could see that the van shoes and boots were tied together by their laces; this was what gave him the idea before he pitched his own into the barrel. His father lifted him up to scan the shoes on the table. *What do you think, Big Ben?* He picked up a black pair, sort of more boots than shoes, but not quite fully boots. *These'd be handy for work.*

Which meant that in a short time their nice black sheen would be disappeared under a crust of dried mud. Work involves walking, lots of it; Benny knows that much. And it takes place after his sisters come home from school, so that they can look after the house and him while their father is out. But next year he, Big Ben, will be off to school. Sometimes he forgets that. Sometimes he wants to forget that such a thing as school is in the world. He would like instead to go to work with his father.

Benny nods yes to the black shoe-boots. And his father buys two pairs of yellow laces. One for his new shoe-boots and a smaller pair – on a second look, Benny sees that they are yellow with a black stripe – for Benny's shoes.

As he looks at those laces now criss-crossing his father's shoes under the table, he knows that he must get his shoes back from the barrel. The laces are on them, and the laces are special and unusual: they look a bit like bees. He runs his fingers down his father's laces, tugging on the parts that seem too tight, and tightening the parts that look sloppy and loose.

Next thing he's being brought up from the world of shoes

under the table, his father rescuing him like the cat he pulled from far down inside the car engine. It is a good feeling, and Benny thinks that the cat must have felt so too.

Effects

I t has taken a while, but now we know a lot of its corners.

The woman who rents it to us, the woman whose father died, we imagine, in the worn chair next to the fireplace, comes around once a fortnight to collect the brown envelope into which our father neatly places notes.

I'm used to rent envelopes ever since leaving the white house with the red roof. And that was five years ago. I was seven, Maeve three and trotting on legs that were still fat and creased from her time as a baby, Benny a pink squit in a blanket. Our father suddenly without money. Our mother still in our world. I remember that we gave some money to the house of the aunt and cousins that gave us a room for those bad empty months when our father didn't have work. After that, with some breaks and disruptions, rent became a feature of a week, like a television programme coming on at the same time, or sometimes a fortnight. Occasionally a month. The awful flat in Ennis took it at the top of every month and I thought that that was because the owner couldn't bear to visit there any more than we could to live in it.

Rent banks your life with the person whose house it really is. You could go along for a good while pretending that it was yours. But suddenly something will remind you that it could all disappear like a draught up a chimney. In the case of this latest house, we have plenty of signs that we're not its true occupiers. And that feels safer. More real, at least. No pretence made by gleaming countertops and mould-stains badly painted over in bathrooms. All those attempts to make you feel like you'd walked into a brand spanking-new place that had been waiting for you and you only. The Newmarket-on-Fergus house had bottles of Parazone under the kitchen sink, a lone Christmas card at the back of a drawer, coins in the cracks of the couch. And, of course, the coat.

At first we have a list of things to ask the woman who owns the Newmarket-on-Fergus house. How do you make the shower work properly? Did a cat live here, because we saw deep desperate scratches on the base of one of the beds? Where is the trapdoor into the loft? Why did you leave all these things behind you, why didn't you clean the place out before you let someone move in? (Of course, we'd never ask that, or at least not as abruptly.) Our father asks about the shower. When that gets a satisfactory answer (we'd been turning the lever too far left and so diluting it down to a dribble) I decide to make Maeve ask about the cat.

She does, saucily, the query coming out like an insult against the owner. Like she's the kind of messy woman who let animals go wild indoors. This is typical of Maeve, but not intended to be nasty: it's just the way her voice climbs up sometimes. High and quavery. It gives the most ordinary of questions a note of outrage or panic.

The woman laughs, which makes us suddenly like her very much. She tuts and says that her father used to keep a *vicious old prowler* in the house. She never saw the tomcat properly, only as a blaze of orange fur running from room to room whenever she came to visit. I ask if his tail went huge and stunned-looking, the way that cats' tails do when they're afraid or angry. I feel like I want to keep her here at the table, talking, telling odd stories about her father and the cat. It makes matters kinder and more liveable, knowing that the old man whose ghostly coat still hung in the hall had a companion, however edgy or destructive.

I ask about the loft. She tilts her head to one side and smiles as if I'd asked her something personal. I feel myself turn red, and shout inside my head to turn the blush down, so that Maeve won't start giggling and pointing. Once she got to know that this was something out of my control, like a fierce spell I could only ward off by closing my eyes and talking loudly silently, it became her weapon. I wasn't invincible any more.

The thing is, I'd never been invincible. My slight limp from when I'd fallen from the top of a wardrobe where I'd climbed to hide at the cousins' those years ago, should have been her target. But there's some kind of decency to my sister, I suppose, and she never once made a mockery of it. At least not the way a handful of tough girls at school did. Girls are always worse than boys. To boys, it's a kind of war wound, which makes you distant, and plucky for getting on with it. However, when it comes to the blushing, Maeve takes her enjoyment.

So I stare into the woman's pleasant blue eyes, cooling myself under their light. They look mesmerizing, like the eyes of a woman in an ad for diamonds or a holiday in Iceland. I tell her that we've always liked lofts. Because you can't get up there very often. And things are stored there to the point of being forgotten, even though they're over people's heads all the time. I tell her about the loft in the flat in Ennis, how we were convinced that we could hear rats skittering across the boards every night at around ten o'clock. How

Benny would show his fear by moving his eyes side to side, me to Maeve to me, gauging if we heard what he heard. She says that there are no rats in our loft, and neither is there anything stored up there. *Are you sure you can't guess where the trapdoor is, hmm?* We want to figure it out, Maeve and I, and put our heads into our hands to map every corner of the ceilings we'd seen. No go. *It's actually in the garage, she says, which is not all that usual. There's hardly any space above it. When my father passed away I went up on a rickety ladder and flapped my hand around in the dark and dust in case he'd left any money up there.*

Maeve puts her hands over her mouth and stuffs a laugh back in. I draw her out, because I want to embarrass her for pointing out the blushing. When she isn't being bold to teachers or picking fights in the playground, my sister can be very funny, though. *It's good that your da didn't keep his money in the mattress, or the old cat would've loved tearing it up.* She mimics a crazy cat shredding stuff and gleefully throwing it into the air.

All three of us are laughing when our father comes back with the teapot in one hand and Benny's sleeve in the other. Benny seems to be pretending he has a broken arm, leaving one sleeve of his pyjamas slack. *Look at this fella, would you. He's like a little soldier.* Our father is in good humour; maybe he likes the sound of laughing in the kitchen, the pleasant woman being friendly to his girls. There's something summery about it, even though it's only February.

When she leaves she goes out by the back door instead of the front as she usually does.

I always like the sound of her car curving into the front, the lights, if it was late enough in the evening, washing glamorously past the sitting-room window. I think it's because I want to believe that it's a real visitor for a change, somebody magical turning up to tell us that we've won a new house and a new car. And a holiday. And spending money, for they almost always gave spending money with holidays nowadays.

But it's always only the woman who owns the house, here to get the envelope.

Maybe this time she intended to stay for tea and stories, though, because she parked at the side of the house and walked around the path to the back door. I was in the bathroom and I heard her steps lightly dinning the concrete. Our father had told us that there was a pipe running under that patch of path, which is why your steps sounded different on it. Echoey and more lively.

She leaves with a flutter of hands – waving kootchy goodbyes to me and Maeve, patting Benny's head, taking the envelope from between our father's fingers. He holds it lightly, nonchalantly, as if were a piece of paper he could as easily let go to the wind. I try to suss them out with the eyes of a child in a film about a father who was divorced or a widower. One of those stories where the child somehow manages to make romantic mischief for the father, and create a potential new mother. I hate those films, especially ones where the adults seem not to recognize how devious the kid is. It's still devious, even if there's a happy resolution; I just don't agree with interfering in grown-ups' lives like that. Our father would never look romantically at this woman he rented the house from. Even if she does have those jewel-like blue eyes. Even if she is close to his age. He would never bother because he was still living something for our mother. You never really saw much of that kind of hanging-on in those romantic films. People are always told, usually by a caring or busybody friend, that it's time to Move On.

The woman stops on her way through the back hall and calls in to us. *Oh Jesus, I didn't know this was still here. I'm so very sorry.* We don't know whether to follow her out there or not. So I push Maeve off her stool and shoo her to see what's happening. I follow at a respectable distance. She has the old coat in her arms; it lays there like an emptied person. She looks down at it like you sometimes see people looking at babies in shawls. *Listen, if there's anything else lying around, anything that you're not happy to use, I don't mind if you make a pile of it and have it taken away. Or burned.* Our father is standing on the threshold, nodding slowly, kindly.

She says she won't take for next month's rent in return for our clearing the house.

I think for a minute or two about whether this is just sheer lazy craftiness on her part. But I prefer to consider that it would be too sad for her. Maybe there are photos of her as a girl somewhere, sitting on her father's knee. His holey old towels. Stuff she'd like not to have to decide whether to keep or throw out. Attachment to things is a terrible burden, and I'm glad we don't have many of them to be fretting about.

But she says we could be in charge of deciding what to hold and what to throw away. There's a garage full of shelves, on them cardboard boxes going soft and mulchy at the corners. Suddenly this seems like an adventure.

Maeve wakes knowing that she dreamt about burning stuff. Heat and frizzle behind her eyes. One of those dreams that she sometimes ends up carrying with her for half the day. Dreams that flash across a morning's multiplication tables and make her turn sharply to whoever's licking their pencil or rubbing things out either side of her. Sure that the panic running through her must be felt along the line of the class like a shock on an electrical fence.

Today is the Saturday morning that their father has set aside for tidying out the old man's stuff. His effects, as he calls them. Effects? she questions him with her eyes across the bowl of softly popping cereal. She's fond of cereal, most of the time. They ate a lot of it for supper two or three years ago. Not, though, Weetabix. She told her father that she wouldn't eat it any more because it tasted like a dried-out piece of dog doo. Complete with the straw and hair you sometimes saw in that. Just when it looked like he would shout the ceiling down, he started laughing and said that that was *the funniest of the disgusting things* he'd heard in his life. But that didn't make it right to say again, *ever*, just so she knew, like.

Gathering and sorting and hopefully burning the old man's stuff will give a bit of action to the day. Saturdays can sometimes hang like the weight of rain in clouds. Saturdays fail her, because she knows that she should be thinking of games to play, but by the time she convinces Eva or drags Benny into whatever her plan is, suddenly she doesn't care any more and the day is as good as over. Saturday feels like the small sister of Sunday: the day nobody wants to do anything with, or the day that gets landed with all the chores.

But today at least they will be looking for effects.

Which she now knows are the personal items belonging to a dead person.

Her father chases the last of his cereal round the bottom of the bowl. He eats the bran stuff that looks and tastes like twigs.

Effects could be something else, though, Maeve thinks. Like the feeling that a person leaves behind them. A feeling that stays like something you can't wrap up or put in a box, a feeling like a smell or taste. The way that your chest feels flattened under a rock when you think of them.

She'd love to tell her father this idea. She thinks he'd appreciate it and sit back to take it in as though he was smoking it. But she's also afraid that it would upset him. She knows what he looks like when certain things catch him out. He gets red blotches, as if some invisible person is pressing fingers and thumbs on his jaw and neck. He turns quiet, so quiet that he could pass the quiz programme and not suggest a single answer. And certainly not shout at anyone in the chair giving their shivery answers, terrified of losing their money because of the colours on the flag of a country.

The only one he might shout at would be the person who

said something to raise the red anger on his face. And so that's why they don't mention any of these things any more. Even Benny seems to know better, and you would think he'd be the most likely one to blurt out things. But Maeve thinks that Benny is too young to have felt the severe changes that she and Eva did, even if he passed through them all the same. Even if he was there that awful night. Poor Benny. Her silent freckled little brother. She thinks there's something magic about him, and something sort of creepy, with it.

She tips the sweet cereal milk back into her mouth and goes out to the garage where Eva has already started studying what they must do.

Very typical Eva, standing with her hands on her hips, giving the idea that she is busy, when Maeve would probably end up doing most of the dirty work. And it would be dirty, for as soon as they budge a box on a shelf they can see the amount of dark dust it hoards round its bottom. The box is damp and rattly and when they open it they see what seems to be a hundred door knobs. All different. Some are even made of pottery. Maeve immediately wants to keep everything in this box, and she has to reason with Eva that they wouldn't burn in a fire anyhow. Their father intervenes, having been watching from the threshold. He tells Maeve that she can keep five of her favourite knobs and no more. Anything that wouldn't burn they would bag and bring to the rubbish dump.

Eva has tied a teatowel round her head like a gypsy's scarf. Maeve wishes that she'd thought of that idea. Even if it looks stupid – the towel is white with brown flowers – it keeps her clean and tidy. Maeve can feel her own hair getting clagged and itchy. But she won't get a towel and do the same, for Eva would mock her as a copycat.

Most of the other boxes don't hoard much worth fighting to

hold onto. There are lots of old magazines that seem to be about farming. They came from America because you can see the price on them, the dollar sign that looks like a musical note. They have photographs of combine harvesters and ploughs on the front. They look thoroughly boring, but Maeve supposes that their father might be interested in this sort of stuff, so she summons him over from his side of the garage where he is picking through old nails and screws to see what ones might still be useful. *I can't understand a man keeping so many bent nails in a jar. Where's the utility in that?* He has shown Benny how to sort the good from the bad, and Benny sits contentedly examining nails at close range, like a jeweller Maeve once saw in a film checking diamonds. Turning them round at all angles.

Her father takes one of the magazines, one that announces The Way of the Future for Forestation. Maeve thinks that this most recent job of his, looking after the trees at Dromoland Wood, must be a pleasant one. Even though he leaves after three o'clock and doesn't come back some evenings until after eight, it seems to balance him out a bit more. He spends the earlier part of the day with Benny, which would calm anybody, and the rest of it among trees and pathways and protected creatures.

She watches him open the magazine and page through it slowly. He walks back to his side of the garage and she knows that he's lost for an hour in whatever out-of-date information the faded magazine contains.

Then Eva bails out, having found a box of old *Reader's Digests*. She wants to read out a story to Maeve, one about a man who gets almost eaten to death by a grizzly bear. She shows her the pencil drawing of a bear looming over a man. Maeve can't believe how detailed the drawing is; even in black and white you can see the points of the grizzly's claws and the bend in the man's trouser knees as he backs away. And you just know he's going to trip on the root of a tree and let the bear have at him. She wants to find out, so she lets Eva start reading.

For someone with such a soft and saintly face, Eva has a real thirst for blood and guts. She likes those programmes about sharks, for example, where the only way people can get to study sharks is to go down in a cage. The shark butts the cage; Eva jumps. She wants to get to the part where someone's leg is bitten off.

Maeve looks across at their father, sitting down now with his legs crossed almost in a figure of eight on the floor. If she lets her eyes go out of focus a little, the way he is sitting makes him look like he has no legs. Like the man she saw in the market in Ennis: in a wheelchair with his trouser legs folded up to the length of shorts, the fabric flat where no legs lay.

Benny still has a lot of work to do with the nails and screws, but he gives it the same serious attention that he does blowing the fluff off a dandelion clock or pretending to count all the animals in the fields across the road and up the hill.

So she gives in and lets Eva start reading. For a while she wants to burst out laughing at her sister's voice. Instead of letting on to be dramatic like the chilly voices on her shark and crime-scene programmes, Eva reads it like Miss Hyland might read the story of Rip Van Winkle. In a low voice, drawing you in with pauses and raised eyebrows. Maeve tries to imagine Miss Hyland reading this grizzly bear story to the class. It feels satisfying to think of everyone running out into the school yard screaming.

But at least the bear story is intended to be frightening. Getting mauled and chewed up is terrifying, there and then as you hear about it bit by bit. The funny thing is, Maeve found the Rip Van Winkle story more alarming. She felt sort of queasy about the idea of sleeping for twenty years and then discovering what everything was like when you came back down from the mountain. She remembers that Rip's wife was mean to him. She heard her father call a woman in a shop a *rap* one time, because she'd pushed past them in the line of trolleys at the check-out. Mrs Van Winkle was a rap, but she was dead when he returned. Every other man is envious of how things worked out for Rip. Maeve didn't like that part at all. It seemed very lousy to the memory of his wife, even if she had been a rap.

Even as it sank its jaws into my head, I could not help but be in awe of this most fearsome of creatures. Due to the blood loss from my arms and the energy lost in trying to fight it, I felt myself slipping out of consciousness, and our fight becoming a gentle dance. The garage is now just Eva's voice and the man's struggle with the bear. Of course he will escape, by some miracle of the bear deciding to let go or someone firing a rifle. The man should not be trying to fight it, anyhow. Best pretend to be dead. Bears get bored with that, it's said. But he writes this so well that you think he might not have survived. It makes her think that it would be good but frightening to be a writer. In the case of this article, the poor bear man probably had to scare himself all over again to write it.

Later she will deny to herself that she saw Benny leave the garage. Nobody else saw him. She can't be the only one. So she must have imagined it.

The man in the bear's mouth starts to remember a long poem he had learned and loved in college. *When lilacs last in the dooryard bloom'd.* It sounds nice, and a good thing to remember at that time. Better than a prayer, maybe. *Song of the bleeding throat.*

On the lowest shelf behind Eva and Maeve, except it's not really a shelf because it's just where the floor is at the bottom of the row, Benny sees the tips of a pair of boots. They sit there like the person wearing them might be hiding flat behind the shelves. The boots and the old coat. Some man used to wear them. He put them on when he was leaving this house to go to work. He sat in their kitchen and unlaced them. Maybe he hissed a bit, like their father does when the back of the boot just will not come free.

To Benny it is all very strange that they are going into boxes and making a pile of that man's things. It makes him feel cold inside his shirt. This is what happens when somebody is not around any more. He tries to follow that thought further. But it feels like going to the corner of the backyard where the outside light can't fully reach. He always turns round and runs back. Dreadful things that might chase a boy live inside the edge of that dark part of the yard. It lies there like a pool of quiet water. He has tried to tell Eva about this feeling, but she just laughed and forced him to watch a shark dragging a person under the water. *That's more likely to happen to you than something taking you in the yard.* Benny wonders why his sister who he hears crying sometimes in the night is not more afraid of what he is afraid of. And why she is not nicer.

He goes back to working on the nails his father asked him to divide into two piles. Bent ones and straight ones. He takes a straight one and tries his hardest to bend it like an elbow. Pushing hard with his thumb does no good. How did they get like this? Why does he have to do this job? Eva and Maeve are sitting with their backs against the shelves reading something. Eva likes to read out loud and he likes the times that she reads stories to him. But not so long ago she had said she was tired of the books that told *stupid romantic stuff* and she did not want to read his favourite one any more. *Snow White and the Seven Dwarves.* She said that she did not know why a boy liked that so much, anyhow. Maeve had laughed and said that the dwarves all looked like Benny and maybe that was why. She went around calling him Doc for a week. Laughing. They laughed at him a lot.

Which is why he could never tell them that it was the part about the glass coffin that he loved so much. The way the dwarves cried when they looked at Snow White inside it. And the way that the piece of poisoned apple came out of her mouth when the glass coffin was bumpily carried along. It seemed like such an easy thing to happen. Especially after all the trouble the stepmother had taken with her evil plans.

And Benny knows just what it feels like. For he himself had a sweet stopping his breath one time. He should not have been eating the sweet; it was one of the big hard mint humbugs that only his father and sisters were allowed to eat. But he found one, unwrapped, on the edge of the bathroom sink. It was as if Maeve or Eva had been about to start sucking it and then decided to brush their teeth instead. And so he put it in his mouth.

He knew that he had done a very wrong thing when he felt it slip from the grip of his teeth. Something that felt ten times bigger than the humbug filled the back of his mouth. Closed off the part where he needed to breathe. It felt like a trapdoor with somebody sitting on it, and Benny trying to push back. He remembers walking as if he was blind and deaf and dumb, out to the kitchen. As if the world was slowly stopping around him. Nobody there. The sitting room. Eva lifting and running with him to their father who was painting the front gate. He remembers the bitter smell of paint on his father's hands, hands turning him over and pushing in a place that felt harsh and painful. The humbug lying wet and shining on the path. Wanting his father to suck the sweet down to the thin black glassy coins that his sisters made of theirs sometimes, then put it back into his own mouth. Because it had tasted nice, in spite of all the trouble. His father was shouting at Eva and Maeve; there would probably be no more humbugs in the house. This was what happened when they had let something dangerous take place. The firelighter that he crumbled into a nice-smelling dust on his lap.

But he had survived the humbug like Snow White had woken up inside the glass coffin with the piece of apple beside her.

And she had a lovely face with very very red lips. They looked like a heart painted on her face.

Benny suddenly feels very cross that Eva will not read the story to him any more. Her voice across the floor makes him push his thumb harder into the head of a nail. He wants to run over and grab whatever she is reading to Maeve and tear out its pages. He would use the nail to do this. It would work well, and it would be frightening. Then he wishes that the pair of boots really did have a hidden man standing in them, a man who would push the shelves down on top of his sisters. He knows that it is very wrong to think of this. But it feels nice, just for a moment. And they would never know that he had wished it.

And then he remembers his shoes.

And how he will get in trouble for throwing them into the barrel.

One of his sisters will find out and tell on him and then their father will turn red and say loud things about the price of good shoes. He must get them back. Now is a good time, because everyone seems to be busy with reading.

Outside seems nicely lit after the garage.

The day is yellower.

Next door's dog is running on the chain; Benny can hear him scouting along inside the fence. Sometimes it sounds like the chain is a noisy tail that the dog wags happily. Other times Benny hears the sound of a bursting run, then a yelp. The dog's disappointment. How horrible it must be to be tied on a chain. Benny thinks that there should be a story about a dog whose wicked owner chains him, but then he gets free and never comes back. The story would end with a picture of the owner standing over the chain coiled up like a snake. His face would be red and confused.

Benny is at the barrel when he realizes that he will need something to help him get the shoes out. Not only that, but he will need to find a way to climb up. Throwing them in was easy; he did not need to be as tall as the barrel to do that. He remembers the metal bucket that his father uses to take out the ashes. He sees Eva's badminton racket under the shrubs. He is pleased at how his plan is working so far.

The upturned ashes bucket is not quite good enough on its own. He gets a piece of firewood from the pile stacked in the barn and puts the flat side on the bucket. It feels nice and round under his feet. Like walking on a rolling pin, which he saw the boys next door do until their mother came out and called them little thugs and bandits. The rim of the drainpipe is rusty. So he does not dare hold onto it, because he has heard all about what rust does to blood from the time Maeve ran in after standing on the lid of a bean can at the back of the barn.

The water is not as creepy during daytime. He can see almost to the bottom. Even though he cannot make out his shoes, he knows that they are there. Waiting to be rescued. He swishes the badminton racket around like a fishing net.

He must rise up on tiptoes.

He needs to lean in more, and digs his elbows into the rim.

The wooden block spins free like a rolling pin and he wonders how those boys stayed on it for so long. His head hits the bottom and he thinks how big and sad and drowned his shoes look.

This time I'm in the passenger seat, instead of sitting in behind the garda. I make a joke about how being in the back seat made me feel like a perp. When he looks at me sidelong, I bite off my attempt at a laugh. I feel that I should explain where I picked up the word. Last year, my first in college, a bunch of us would watch old episodes of Hill Street Blues *at midnight. I don't confess to the garda my embarrassing crush on Lt Frank Furillo and how I hated every minute he spent in the bubble bath with Joyce Davenport.*

So I just tell him about how I followed the programme until the late-night repeats stopped abruptly and were replaced by a music series. And he makes chat for the first time all morning, asking if I've ever seen a film called Assault on Precinct 13 and how it's the fiercest thing altogether.

I watch him covertly as he talks; his face is that long slightly doleful face that I've come to associate with gardaí. Only because I've never seen one with a round chubby-cheeked face. I went out with one for a time — a trainee — and so did my housemate Linda when she met my fella's friend. Both of them would arrive at the door looking as professionally melancholy as funeral directors. They even stood with their hands clasped in front of them. It turned out that they worked nights on door security at a nightclub. Linda used to say that going out with The Law was the only thing keeping us from a life of drugs and general looseness. We synchronized our break-ups with them — Linda's idea — so that they would be able to console each other and talk evenly and squarely, dumped man to dumped man, about what bitches we were.

I wonder how she'll take it when I tell her later about where I disappeared to this morning.

Then, as unexpectedly as he started, my garda cuts off talking about Precinct 13 in order to concentrate on the road. It's slow and torturous going, with sometimes only a ragged ribbon of asphalt between the car and the gorse.

He must be wondering how people live this far from decent roads.

Why my father would have elected to do so.

I want to tell him about the time he decided to bike up a treacherous hill that he'd heard about in Clare. And, in his version of events, spun into the margin and slid many feet on his hip before coming to rest against a bush growing at a bend. The thing was, he and the bike were still joined in a deadly lock, for it was a racer he'd bought years ago, and he insisted on fastening his feet into those pedal cages.

I only heard this story some months after the accident. And it seemed like something from a cartoon. I could imagine him taking the bike up the hill alright, tilting side to side like the professional racers do. Far left, far right, the only means by which you can attack a steep slope. He used to watch the cycling tours, a favourite part being the madness of trying to take on Patrick's Hill in Cork city.

He liked the dramatic extremes involved in many sports. If it was soccer, then he'd be up for a penalty shoot-out. Loving the tragedy of the greatest players cracking and sending it over the bar. Roberto Baggio with his hands to his face. Incidents and accidents. I remember him telling me about the boxer who had sent another man into a coma in a knockout and how that coma had lasted six months and the boxer had died in his home country of Nigeria. It struck me that he, whose only pursuit was his solitary cycles, needed the prospect of something drastic in order to sustain his interest in other sports. I once asked him if he would watch a fox-hunt, thinking that his thirst for blood might extend to animal sporting. Are you out of your mind, are you? I'd sooner shoot every last one of them up on the horses. Fat Big House bastards. Redcoat cunts. *Then he caught himself, stunned at the words and at my pale face.* No. Ah no. I'd watch greyhounds running alright. But nothing chasing after something defenceless. *He was working on the grounds of Dromoland Castle then. I was instantly ashamed of my question. Because he used to come home talking about creatures he'd seen and tried not to startle, like red squirrels,* which they say are dying out *and nests of rabbits* just like a heaving hive of fur *and grouse and pheasants and all sorts of small elegant birds.*

We're moving at what seems less than ten miles an hour. I have a most dreadful urge to turn on the radio. But that wouldn't seem right, given the circumstances, and I don't want to be the brunt of a reproachful glance from my driver.

I could go through the notebook, I suppose. It sits snugly in my coat, one of those made particularly for a pocket. A reporter's notebook.

But it's sealed shut under the sticky cellophane. I run my fingernail along the edge where the cover overlaps the pages, searching for a pocket of air. That cellophane, in spite of the best efforts at smoothing it, stroking it like a cat that needed firm love, always trapped air in a bubble on our schoolbooks. Sometimes it would just be pimple-sized, other times it would stand out like a big raised weal. That used to infuriate me, and I would take a needle to it. It was as silently satisfying as bursting a blister. Along the edge of the notebook I find what looks like a possibility. But I have nothing to prod it with. A house key is too thick. I take off my earring, trying to do so without the garda seeing.

There's no reason why I should care if he does. But there's something about him that suggests a reproof to everything. It's why I pressed the box of cigarettes as flat as I could in my pocket when I sat into the passenger seat.

Inside me flares an angry suspicion that he'd be quick to judge that I'm not taking these events seriously enough. I bet he's from the deepest countryside, one of those places that produce the most severe none-of-your-messing gardaí. So I take pleasure in thinking Fuck You very slowly and loudly in my head, the way a gangster would drag it out as one final insult before he's about to be shot. And then I get to work on the notebook.

The prong works well to make a rent in the cellophane. I wiggle it along slowly until I have enough open to begin tearing. It comes apart reasonably neatly, and I feel irrationally proud of that. Perhaps because it was sealed so neatly. Ripping and tearing messily would have seemed sacrilegious or something.

My hands set up trembling when I see my father's handwriting. Lettering that I used to think was disorderly until realizing that it was as innate and unchangeable as your own soul. Everyone having a different signature, from the neatly rounded and legible to the theatrical scrawl. In college I figured out the best people to borrow notes from on the basis of handwriting; I'd go for the wilder style because I associated it with cleverness. I wasn't always right about that. But it was a great way to learn the material of the lectures, as deciphering the handwriting took ages and you ended up absorbing the notes into your system that way. My father's name huddles in the top right of the blank first page. First name above surname. It was as if his lone first name, those five letters, seemed naked or foolish and childish, and he had to hurriedly add the surname for foundation and support.

Flicking forward I see that it's a notebook he has fashioned into a diary: dates are added in his hand at the top right. I thumb back until I see August 1995. A panic clatters round in my chest. I think of the hens' alarm and hope they're alright for the time being. I didn't even check to see if they had food. After August 1995 we weren't allowed to talk about sad close things. That was when our father started the business of forgetting. But there on the first date is a drawing in blue biro of the first home I remember, the house with the red roof. We didn't live there *in 1995, we hadn't lived there for a while, but our father was reliving its corners on that page. He drew the windows with double frames around them and he had a driveway snaking out from the front door. Written underneath it in heavy emphatic letters:* First house, Newcastle, Galway. Happiest time.

Happiest. The word lances me like a cursed word. He wrote this. To write it he must have believed in it. He must have spent time returning there and savouring the faint taste of that time that I could only con myself into remembering as real.

And that's why I feel like opening the window and throwing this diary out, like my sister once did with a beloved red-haired Victorian doll of mine. I want it to be lost to the gorse and melted away under dirty rain. It feels bigger in my hands; it threatens to open and flap out its pages noisily. He kept a diary. After all we'd been forced to learn about forgetting. The four of us are the world now, and the world moves forward every day. *Maeve getting sent away from the table crying when she shouted our mother's name. Out of nowhere it came, then over and over. First of all I thought it was funny.* Belinda Belinda BelindaBelindaBelinda. *Until the name turned into a whirl* BlindaBlndaBln *and then the smack from our father, sudden as a pistol shot, that stopped her tongue in its gallop.* What did I tell you girls? WHAT did I TELL you? *Benny shrinking back against our father's shirt, as though the big voice was coming from outside the house somewhere and he needed protection from it. I thought about leaving the table with Maeve but I didn't have the guts.*

And because I didn't it must have seemed like I fell in with our father's orders. Maeve and I never mentioned our mother to each other after that.

I don't want to go any deeper into this diary.

I'm afraid of the hypocrite that'll come crawling out of it.

Like silverfish from the pages of an old medical textbook from the college library. Live slivers on my hands. I shouldn't have smacked them, but I did, and crushed them to sardine scales.

I don't know if he drew the house of the happiest time before or after she died. It happened in the middle of that August.

The car slows to a complete stop and I look up. We're flanked either side by sheep streaming along the road. They press against the car, jostling each other like kids pouring through a school gate. At close range I can see how grey their coats are, how tightly whorled the wool. Nice old creatures. *The garda is appreciative, which makes me think he doesn't come from sheep-farming people. Linda, whose brothers wrangled sheep into dips and through fences when they got wedged, once told me how they roped her into helping them, and how the sheep were most vicious in their resistance.* Belligerent animals, absolutely belligerent. You won't get more awkward than a sheep, even when you're trying to help it. *But for now, as our car gently rocks like a boat in the middle of their press and bustle, I'm preferring to believe the garda.*

And I know that I can't put the diary away when the car picks up the journey again. There's a while before we get into town and I do what I have to do there. There's my father in these pages and my father gone from the burned house and maybe if I get some guts I'll find out what happened to make him into one, and then the other.

I riffle along the tops of the pages for more dates. They cover many years, but there are big chunks of time missing. The pages are light, almost as thin as Rizzla paper. I close them for a moment, using my finger as a marker. The car is stuffy. The steamy aftermath of sunshowers and the car itself, which smells like socks and old aftershave.

If Maeve were with me, would she prod me along to find if there was anything written about the day Benny went into the barrel? She never let him out of her sight once he came back to us. And he needed all that care because he was never the same again. The last time I saw them both was eating ice-cream cones in Salthill. They'd taken the bus to see me after my exams finished.

Going off to college is a breaking with family for most people. A small number of my friends hardened that into entire semesters of never going or phoning home. Others, like Linda, would bundle themselves, bags first, onto the bus to Donegal every Friday. The Long Haul, *as she called it, in mock exasperation. But I knew she loved heading off. I imagined her father or mother waiting for her in a car-park near the station, the car lights on and dimmed, like big friendly eyes there to greet her. She'd return last thing on a Sunday night. Laundry done and crisply folded like something from an old-style draper's shelf. Often a casserole. She could've made it last a couple of days, but she always heated and shared it on Monday evening. I knew she sometimes picked up little things in the city for her mother and sisters. This exchange of lipsticks and casseroles seemed the most fluid and natural thing in the world. I was in awe of it.*

I wonder what it was like when my garda left home for training. I sneak a look at his profile and imagine a tall long-chinned mother standing sadly at the back door in a big stone farmhouse. One of those August nights when the sudden drop into darkness means that autumn is clipping along fast; she'll have gathered her open cardigan to herself and turned into the kitchen.

Imagining other people's families has become an elaborate pastime for me.

When Maeve and Benny turned up without warning, I couldn't take it in. It was a Saturday, and Maeve would have known that I tended to take most of the first part of the day for lolling in bed. Around eleven I heard steps and voices advancing on my bedroom door; Gráinne flung it open; in she ushered my sister and brother. My first instinct was to wish that Gráinne had been out. She and I were only on the brittlest of terms. I considered her judgmental — a wagon, in Linda's word — and I wanted to throw a cloak over Maeve and Benny to protect them from her bitchily amused gaze. I got dressed at top speed and made an excuse about the house being untidy when Maeve wanted to look around. As we left I saw Gráinne make a quick study of Benny. She had a beady eye and a mouth prone to pursing and I couldn't imagine her as a nurse. Except, of course, of the Ratched variety.

Maeve chatted over her shoulder about the bus driver who wouldn't believe that she was fifteen and tried to charge her more money. In the end Benny started shouting about going home. Perhaps it was my brother's face, like a perplexed angel, that had the driver wave them past at two for the price of one child's ticket. I wanted to ask if she'd gotten permission for this trip. But then I didn't really want to know. I didn't want to have to make a phone call if they'd absconded. More than likely Maeve had wheedled for permission. She was good at that. She might've insisted that it would be good for Benny. The seaside and his beloved oldest sister.

Except Benny didn't really feel like that about me. It was all Maeve. Because I had left for college and he just didn't understand. His world must've seemed like one upheaval after another. Bags and boxes packed, car doors closing, Goodbye, goodbye, be back soon.

She and he walked ahead of me hand in hand. I lived near Salthill then, so it didn't take us long. Maeve had the practised walk of someone used to steering Benny past people and baby buggies and through traffic. I had an urge to take his other hand, but I was afraid that he'd shake it off as though it burned. Plus he was nearly eleven. I had to remember that.

People would stare.

People loved to stare.

Their eyes widened to taste whatever looked a bit out of the ordinary. Like Gráinne, they'd hoard away the image of the boy with the rolling eyes and his sister with the light limp and his other sister who was so gorgeous that there was something nearly criminal about it. They'd think about it later in the day as though it was a postcard they'd seen on a stand outside a shop.

And now I wonder if the garda noted my limp. And if he were a detective would he be able to tell from my footprints that I had one. Sherlock Holmes bending to the marks of soles in the mud and pronouncing that the perpetrator had a limp because of the distinctive impression of the right sole. Elementary.

That day Benny came wanting cones cones cones. Like it's all he'd ever heard about Galway. Like the way people go to Paris for the Eiffel Tower. We found a van playing that eerie hurdy-gurdy music and he watched the ice cream slowly spiral out of the machine. He was glazed with joy. We got chocolate flakes and pink sprinkles. Whatever there was to put on a cone I would get it for them. Because I was gripped by how much I missed our little planet. I could barely put the cone to my mouth for fear I'd cry all over it. Maeve sat on the other end of the bench, regarding the sea and beyond it the low spread of Clare's stone hills. She said, They look like they were poured out and sort of went flat like a cake. I saw what she meant, and I thought it was a very artistic way of noticing stuff. It wasn't just that she noticed it, but that she said it out loud, unashamed. Maybe she would become a writer, like I used to want to be.

Maybe she would be devouring this diary right now. She wouldn't be afraid of things from the heart, whether happy or sad or painful or shaming.

In total they stayed for three hours. After the cones we walked along the strand. I stayed Benny's hand when he picked up a pebble and tried to lob it at a seagull. He gave me a vexed look. But because it came from under the most golden eyebrows you could imagine, I had to smile. We went to a lunch place that I knew from meeting a college boy there earlier in the term. It wasn't the fanciest, but I could tell they loved its plastic tablecloths patterned with daffodils and the fact that one woman seemed to run the whole show. She was Greek and motherly and she kissed Benny on the face — oh my! uh-oh! Maeve and I glanced dread across the table — but he loved it. She brought him into the kitchen to collect our sandwiches and he brought them out one by one, looking as serious as an altar boy carrying a chalice.

As we ate I framed questions for Maeve. How are things at the house and are they still as nice to you two and have there been more visits to our father and is he still working down the time until he thinks we can all live together again.

For it was different when I was part of the equation.

All three of us. Taken into the home of our grandparents. And their friendly dogs that wore themselves out chasing invisible things at night and came home flaffing with satisfaction. It was a comfortable house with soft leather seats and a smell of heather in the big bedrooms. But I suppose it was the calm that I couldn't get used to. So I'd find excuses to fight with Maeve. Clothes I'd pretend went missing. Television programmes on the other channel I said I wanted to watch. Anything to raise a bit of trouble and bring our grandparents scuttling in. Their tender attempts at being firm and no-nonsense-now *only stoked me more.*

When I left for college, it wasn't like I was leaving anything important. Except for my sister and brother, of course. There was no back door to gaze back at as though it would heartbreakingly close on me forever; I didn't linger in the bedroom that never felt like mine. I had lived there for three years. I left the place as easily as if only three strokes of the clock had passed. I wanted to fashion myself into an easy-come, easy-go person, because I thought that was how you got by.

I'm ashamed to think that I used those words to the garda I broke it off with. Ashamed of saying it, that is, not of ditching him.

I didn't ask Maeve anything. She chewed her sandwich carefully and reminded Benny to do the same when it looked like he might gloff the second half. Funny how she noted he was winding up to do just that: taking a big gulp of his lemonade and following it with a deep breath. Exactly what he used to do as a small child. He'd have things out neatly on his tray: the plastic plate of mashed potatoes, peas, and fish fingers cut up in little orange crumby segments. The plastic spoon beside it. The plastic cup with the perforated lid. He'd loft the cup and suck on it noisily like an old man with a tobacco pipe. Sigh with satisfaction. Then dunk his hands into the food, all the better to bring as much as possible to his mouth.

Oh Benny Benny Benny.

With my elbows on the plastic daffodils I started to cry. It broke over me like the waves outside would later drown the rocks when the wind whipped up. I couldn't get control of it and I couldn't look up. Arms came round me and I smelled the kitchen. The Greek woman was warm and capacious. She drew Maeve and Benny to us.

As if to make up for the embarrassment, I hailed a taxi to bring them to the station so they wouldn't miss the bus. We didn't hug because it just wouldn't be the thing to do after the clamber of arms and the long time spent round me in the restaurant. Benny waved at me through the back of the taxi. Probably told to by Maeve. And I had to smile because it looked like the dismissive wave of a celebrity to the paparazzi. His head was lowered and he wafted his hand high in the air. At the last minute Maeve rolled down the window and leaned out to blow a kiss. My sister and brother. Film stars with ice cream spots on their clothes.

I walked back to the house making plans to go back to see them soon. They wouldn't have to get a bus here again. No more bickering with grumpy bus drivers. That's total bullshit, I said aloud. An old man walking his dog looked at me worriedly. Probably thought I was on drugs.

Then, to myself, I'm bullshit. The reason they'd visited was because I'd put off going back every weekend for a long time. I let them down by leaving them to their own devices with our grandparents. Nice people, as kind as you could get. There was no mistaking that. They tried so hard to make family easy for us, they tried in spite of all the troubles under the water. They were nice, but I was still a deserter.

Later today I will have to go to Maeve's school to tell her. And then we will go to Benny's. I'm not sure if he'll know what we mean. The dread of telling them looms worse than going to the garda station. I'll need this garda to stick with me all day.

As if he hears my thoughts he looks at me quickly, more a scan than a look, and nods a pressed smile at the window.

Maeve would want to find what the diary says about Benny.

She'll have her time with it, though, and so I take my bookmarking finger out and return to the very first page. It's dated July 1986. Half a year before I was born.

I once read a book that began with words something like:

This is the last statement of a condemned man and all its words are true.

I am not about to be hanged but I will borrow his words and start this record with the intention that everything in here will be accurate. I will not lie to myself about anything. It would be good to be able to stick to this promise.

Adare, 1994

Money and Cousins and Fish

The lawns of Adare are so bright green it's like they're painted. We arrive in July. The grass of Adare must have drunk all the rain of May and June to look this fresh and healthy.

The green in front of our house in Galway always looked green from a distance. But when you stepped into it and looked deeply you saw it as an older green, darker and flattened. Sometimes there were bald brown patches. Strange places that looked shaved and nothing would ever grow there again. The boys used those patches as a desert for their soldiers.

We drive to the home of our mother's sister. I have only met her once. Because I heard it whispered bitterly by my father, I know that she does not like him. *Your sister never thought I was good enough. She'll love this.* Love *it. The fact that I couldn't keep a house in Galway or hold a job to save my life.* That was how I found out why we had to pack up and leave. *Oh she'll love this.* Maybe she liked him a long time ago. I have seen her smiling in the wedding album. She looked thrilled to be there, so so happy that her sister was getting married. And if she looked that happy, then she must have liked my father some bit.

I don't know what happened to turn her into the woman hissed and spat out in my father's angry words. I understand how the job and the house are connected: if he didn't have one, then it was hard to have the other. So perhaps my aunt knows something more about how he lost his job than I do.

I remember the evening it happened. Maeve and I were hustled up the stairs to play. *Play what?* we looked at each other. Most of our toys were down in the front room. Our mother steered us by our shoulders. Her bump jostled between us and the feeling made me want to laugh. We had a baby on the way. We didn't know what it was — *What make of a baby,* as the ancient man Mister Carey next door put it. *What make of a baby are ye hoping for, girls?* We thought about this separately and both blurted out *boy* at the same time, surprising each other with the strength and loudness of the wish. But then, on the night that our father came home and shouted the house down, the baby was still under lots of layers: our mother's jumper, blouse, the tight thick skin of her belly, and something underneath that again that I thought must be like the shell of an egg.

Upstairs we tried to pluck what words we could from the distance of the kitchen. Or I did, mostly, for Maeve soon lay down on her bed and put the pillow over her head. I figured out that it was something to do with his job, for I heard some people's names that belonged to his work. Seamus who was the boss. Robin who worked with him when they made gardens and rockeries and curving cobbled paths for the new houses. Some trouble had happened between them and now our father was cursing. *No I will not go back to the fucker.* I shrank back from the banisters on the landing. *I will not lower myself. Cap in hand. Just the kind of thing he's expecting, too.*

When our mother started crying I knew it was time to stop

listening. Even though it wasn't loud crying you still knew it was happening. Silence. Then the end of crying, in a few soft yelps like a puppy gulping. I couldn't stand it when she cried, and I was glad that Maeve had fallen asleep. With the pillow still over her head. Which frightened me for a second; maybe she had accidentally smothered herself. I crept over and waited for a sign. She was so still. It felt like watching a picture. Then a tremor went through her, rippling her arm and leg. She was alright.

Maybe we would all be alright.

Fathers could go out in the city and get jobs all the time, anywhere: that's what I thought.

Until he was there to pick me up from school every day. This went on and on. I got used to the hard dry grasp of his hand crossing the road. And I wished that it would end and he would go back to work.

Then very soon it was Christmas. Maeve still believed in Santa; I let on that I did too. Santa brought so many toys and games it was as if he was never ever coming again. If I had known, if I could have stopped him somehow. But he went beyond what we had hoped for and filled the front room with enough presents for all the kids on the estate. Our father had spent the money for our house on Christmas things. I heard this one night when they didn't know I was in the bathroom under the stairs and they were in the hallway. I'd eaten too much of Mister Carey's dense black Christmas cake. I even drank the whiskey he poured for me in a small glass when Maeve and I went to visit him at five o'clock. In the small bathroom I tried to hold back the sounds of my stomach moaning and threatening.

What are we going to do. What are we going to do. Oh Jesus we're in awful trouble.

I felt afraid that our mother's efforts to choke back her crying would be felt by the baby and it wouldn't want to be born.

But it did, a week after that. Benny came on New Year's Day. Our father was lit and shiny pink with happiness. *Would you believe it. A new baby for the New Year. This means great things. This baby is bringing lorryloads of luck with it.* Robin had come round to the house to have a celebration drink with him. Robin was from Wales or Scotland and I thought he was like a young handsome uncle. He even brought sweets for Maeve and me. Quality Street, which I hated, but it was the thought and the fact that he had wrapped them. He tried to persuade our father to come back to work on the gardens with him. He spoke softly and evenly, like a nice priest making sure you understood what different sins and penances meant. He even pulled me over to the table and said, *Will you talk some sense into this man, Eva, will you.* I felt mute and flushed at the suddenness of his hand on my wrist.

But Robin left looking more disappointed than someone should look when a New Year's baby has just arrived.

And he loaned money for four months of payments to the bank when baby Benny didn't bring a lorryload with him.

I knew this because I was in the kitchen drying plates when Robin turned up at the back door. Our father was out on a river walk with Maeve. Our mother had Benny at her breast. His little muzzle pucked against her like a puppy trying to burst a balloon. I didn't want to watch but I couldn't help myself all the same. When a loud knock sounded at the door I almost let the plate flip out of my hands. Robin let himself in and our mother jumped to turn her back and fasten her buttons. Robin blushed like mad; even his forehead had a flame down the middle.

I was surprised that they let me continue drying the dishes while they talked. It seemed that they forgot I was there. And indeed that Benny was there. He lay on the kitchen table until a whimper from him made our mother say, *O! Jesus!* and scoop him up. The talk was serious. A bit like an argument, without being vexed. They talked like old friends who could not agree on something and were trying to be gentle with each other about it. And that was money. Robin had brought it. *To tide things over.* His voice made it sound like a blessing. In the end, after I had dried the plates for a second time, and dragged the edge of the towel between the prongs of the forks, our mother said yes. Robin put his hand on her shoulder; he looked happy and relieved. I knew what Robin's hand felt like. And for a second I was jealous of our mother's shoulder, wondering if it felt hot and pleasant under his grip.

She would only accept the money as a loan.

She would only accept the money if she could pretend it came from her own brother. Who lived in England. Who transferred the money into her bank account. Did Robin follow this? *It's the only way this will work and you and him will stay friends. And I think that's important.*

I was stunned at her plan. It was both sly and very caring. For she was fond of the friendship. And she wanted our father to return to work with Robin. The money could make a lot of trouble if it wasn't hidden. I thought about the Trojan Horse we read about in our history book. Of course, that was a pretend gift used for a war. But the idea was still great.

And I was sure she wanted to stay friends with Robin, too. She had to want to. He was so lovely and kind. Everything would be alright because he had made it that way. He had brought the lorryload of luck. Then he leaned over and fixed the buttons on her blouse that she had done up wrong. I turned away and felt her watching me for the first time since he had arrived. I hauled the plug out of the sink and let the water spiral down in a loud monstrous suck. Robin left by the back door, stopping to rub his knuckles on my head.

I kept my eyes on the last of the grey foam disappearing in the sink.

Not a word about this, Eva. It's the only way things will work.

And I nodded and nodded. To let our mother know she could trust me totally. Not a word about the money or the lie about her brother. Not a word about the friendship. Not a word about the buttoning of the blouse.

Our father ranted and raved about our mother's brother in England and who did he think he was and what kind of charity cases did he think we were. But our mother stood her ground and said that the money came to her bank account and so she would use it for the house payments. There was something about holding Benny over her shoulder and patting his back for wind that made her more powerful when she spoke. *I am doing this and there's nothing you can do about it.*

End of story.

Until the money ran out. And our father hadn't found a job, and hadn't signed for social welfare. *I'm not a grubber. I won't rely on the State.* His proud voice sounded useless and embarrassing. Like a ringmaster hollering to four people in a circus.

And not long after that we moved to Adare.

Our mother made the announcement with Benny's mouth clipped to her nipple. She used to be shy and modest about the feeds. But she wasn't any more, and she spoke across the table in a low heartbreaking voice. Benny sucked with his eyes closed. His hand outside the blanket flexed like a spider thinking about whether or not to land.

We drive to Adare on a hot Sunday. I don't look back as the car pulls away from the green for the last time. I know someone is on the swing and I can't stand to see their happy flight towards the thick leaves. Robin follows our car with a van full of boxes and the pieces of furniture that belonged to us and not the house with the red roof. Out on the main road I turn round to him every so often. Once or twice I drag Maeve's hand up and pretend to wave it. I'd like to have a notebook to write messages in big letters to him.

A THOUSAND MORE MILES.

ONLY JOKING.

MAEVE WANTS TO MARRY YOU.

Our father starts a game of I Spy.

Something beginning with C. *Cow!* Maeve shouts. But I see the caravan pulled in from the road ahead of us. I get to pick the next one. I think I could do G for gypsies or T for Travellers or P for poor people. And that could be all of us in this car, and not just whoever is in the caravan. Instead I do R for Robin and they don't get it for ages because none of them thinks to spy behind them.

We drive around a big house painted pink with red window frames. Our aunt's house looks like a cake. We will live in some part of it, and I wonder what colour that will be.

Maeve does not like the blue room. Most definitely not. It's a very big room, with two wide beds and two tall wardrobes that stand like hulking monsters against the wall. It looks like two rooms made into one, the way that everything on one side has its match on the other. The ceiling is high and patterned, with a white flower in the centre where the light hangs down. It is neat and tidy and they will have to keep it that way since it is not really theirs.

But it is blue.

And blue makes her feel cold. The paint on the walls is shiny. She has to rub it to check that it's not wet. That's how shiny it is. It feels like standing inside what the swimming pool would look like with all the water sucked down the drain. Nobody wants to sleep in a place like that.

But they will all be in there together, so she supposes that will make it feel warmer. Her father showed her how breathing out makes warm steam; he blew on the window of the car to prove it. But then again you can breathe out clouds like that in cold weather too. She had seen it on their river walks. It looked like her father was smoking inside his hood, but he was not because he stopped that just before Benny was born. The fog danced from his mouth because it was cold. She watched her own breath gather in front of her; she walked through it expecting to feel something like Eva's First Communion veil brushing her face. But she felt nothing.

From the top of the stairs the cousins watch them walking round the bedroom. They watch them carry all their stuff in. They say nothing and they offer no help. Robin pushes past them, through them, very easily. Especially since they were boys, and they were older, you would think they might offer to carry something. Robin looks crossly at them, at the way they just stand there against the wall. He doesn't care about what they thought because he is not related to them. And he doesn't have to live with them.

Maeve wishes that Robin was coming to live with them too. He would know how to handle these boys. For already Maeve can see that they might be mean. She has never met them before. That's a pity, because then maybe they would be nicer and more welcoming. Glad to see them coming to stay. Happy to have new people to play with.

Paudge has hair shaved so short that it looks dark grey, and he is Eva's age. He has freckles across the tops of his cheeks. Not the usual kind of freckles, not like Ailbhe with the red hair who used to play with Eva. Ailbhe's face looked like shadows from the leaves on the tree on the green were always on her face. Paudge's are more like neat dots drawn by someone. You could join them together and make pictures. Just as she thinks maybe she could draw a frog from the dots he sees her looking and says, *What are you staring at?* She jumps back. She would like to leap up into Robin's arms. Her father cannot save her from the meanness because that might make her mother angry. They must be nice to everyone in this house. Even Paudge.

His brother is older and he has a square face like a man's. He has much longer hair. It trails down past his ears and makes his face look even squarer. It comes down in a dark triangle at his forehead. Maeve thinks it looks like Count Duckula's hair. He might be alright. So far he has only watched the boxes passing him, standing solidly with his arms folded. He's the one who should be offering to help, and he's the one that Robin looks at with annoyed blue eyes.

Stiofán. She likes his name better than Paudge but she knows it will be harder to say properly. And people don't like when you get stuff like that wrong. Ailbhe used to shout at her, *It's AL-VA not AL-BA!* People were very particular about things, such as names and places and cars and money.

Maybe when she starts school she will be better at names.

But before that there are other important things to be done. Like getting used to this house and the cousins. And the aunt and uncle who have just arrived in a car. Maeve saw her aunt back when Benny was born, when she blew into the house like a gust of wind in a yellow coat and scooped up Benny in such a sudden manner Maeve thought she was about to run back out with him. But that was her way with many things she did. That evening of her visit she began clearing the dinner plates like a race against time. Then she went round the house and collected all the towels and rammed them into the washing machine. Maeve's mother turned red and went to the front room with Benny.

And now here they all are at this aunt's house bringing the last of their stuff in from the car while she and her silent bald husband unpack their car of shopping bags. Maeve watches them take in four bags each, and there are still more in the back seat. So much food. Maybe the cousins eat like farm animals. She worries about how she and her parents and sister and brother will manage if there are boys like this prowling round. Always eyeing the cereal packets and drinking milk straight from the carton. Eva used to do that until she was caught: the chocolate on her mouth printed brown stains on the cardboard spout. Now they knew that it was rude and it might spread germs. She definitely did not want Paudge and Stiofán's sloppy mouths on her family's milk carton.

Her aunt's husband is still silent, after all the unpacking and putting away is done, and everyone, and Robin, stands round the kitchen. It's a time for tea to be made and biscuits shaken from a packet onto a plate. But Maeve sees no sign of her aunt making that happen. Maybe the husband – who she should probably think of as her uncle – is dumb. But of course that couldn't be; she has never seen an adult person who couldn't talk. She knew brothers on their estate who could neither hear nor talk. They used their hands, and they always seemed to be telling stories where their fingers braided together or walked or fanned out cards. Sometimes they made noises. Eva said that it sounded like cats stuck inside a freezer. Maeve thought that was horrible.

Then it turns out that the husband-uncle isn't dumb; he just waits a long time before he says stuff. And when he does he won't shut up. This first evening she's trapped in the kitchen, they all are, with his talk of how *Adare has a council of people who make sure the town is looking its best*. At least Robin can leave, and he does, and she feels so sad when she watches him take Benny's little finger and shake it like it is his hand. Maybe they will never see Robin again. He brought laughing with him every time he visited, but now he is gone back to Galway in his white van with the purple furry dice hanging in the front.

Then the cousins start to copy his voice. They make his words sound foolish, as if they spill all over the place and he can't keep control of them. It worries Maeve that they start his as soon as Robin has left, but it frightens her more that her aunt and the husband-uncle say nothing to make them stop.

Maeve looks at Eva to try and guess what she is thinking. It's not too hard: her sister's face is tight and square. She too knows that there is trouble coming round the corner. Only Benny seems content. He's on a bottle now, and their mother nudges the teat round his lips to make them open for it. Maeve doesn't remember her having to do this when she was feeding him from her open shirt. He went to that like he knew exactly what was good for him.

Someone new.

Benny knows this because the smell is different.

Not milky sweet.

Or salty when he puts his mouth on the finger.

The new person lifts him a different way.

He lies on his belly on this person's arm and they move him round and he sees things differently.

But it is uncomfortable because his chin is on this person's hand.

And he feels like he might fall off.

Then he zooms toward cloudy light.

And a smell that makes him want to be somewhere else. Held by someone he knows.

Something is moving inside the dirty light.

The arm brings Benny to it.

And he feels very afraid because something moves in there so quickly.

Swish.

It comes to see him and it has big round eyes and it disappears.

Swish.

He does not like whatever moves in there.

So he does the only thing that will work.

He cries loudly.

Even though it hurts him to do this too much.

The person does not take him away soon enough.
The person waits until he cries a bit more.

Benny feels afraid afraid afraid until hands he knows take him and he smells something he knows.

Falling

A summer has passed in the Adare house. We've found where we like to play in the back lawn: at the end, inside the wall, there's a willow tree. It dangles like pale whispering hair around us. Maeve brings her dolls down there; I read a book while she plays and puts them chatting nonsense to each other and back to her. She reminds me of Ailbhe's granny who lived in her house and used to blather silly things to Ailbhe and her brothers. And to me, I suppose, since I was there too sometimes. But they weren't allowed to laugh at her. As Ailbhe said, *She has lost her mind and we have to talk to her like what she says is normal.*

Our cousins don't follow us to the bottom of the lawn. It's as if the tree is a girly tree and they'd rather be up in the branches of an oak figuring out how to make a tree-house. Our mother sometimes brings Benny down and we sit on a blanket. The kitchen window is like a square eye watching us.

And I wonder if our aunt is in there, looking out to see what we're doing. Sometimes she comes into a room where we are, looks at us, looks around, and then leaves. She doesn't really know what to do with this many extra people, and so she keeps them separate. Sometimes we all eat together, like on Sundays, but most other evenings our mother puts our meals on the table before our aunt and uncle and the cousins take their dinner. This rushes our meals, and I always feel a bit sad when I see Maeve chasing the last pea or lick of soup. Drinking her milk like a calf not wanting to let go of a bucket.

But sometimes when we gather under the willow tree it can feel like we are its real owners and the people in the dark of the house are just the visitors.

Things are starting to settle into a routine. Our father has taken a job: driving a truck for our uncle's company. Our uncle owns a sawmill and he needed one more driver on the road delivering wooden fences and garden sheds. Our father leaves the house earlier and gets home earlier than our uncle, so you'd never think they worked in the same place. Our uncle wears a shirt and tie and carries a case; our father wears a thick blue shirt with the sawmill's name on the pocket.

I wonder if he misses Robin and the laughs they used to have after work some evenings. Sitting on the front wall joking about their boss. Sitting in the kitchen drinking bottles of beer.

And I wonder if our mother has spoken to Robin since the day he helped us to move. She has the use of the house telephone, offered by our aunt in the same way she offers most things. *By all means use it if you need to. We try not to stay on it too long in this house.* But I haven't heard her ring anyone.

Soon I will be starting a new school. The hot days of August will dribble away and cooler duller school weather will arrive. There is a kind of sad rain that I connect with the end of August. It comes as if it's been holding in for as long as it could. Letting kids enjoy themselves for as long as possible. Then it breaks. And it's time to cover new schoolbooks with sticky plastic and try on new shoes.

This year I don't have new shoes. Our mother said that the scuff on the ones bought last August could be sponged back to black with that stuff that smelled like nail polish.

Overall, I'm not too worried about starting the new school. Because last year going back to my own school after summer was like starting somewhere new anyhow. It seemed like everyone had changed in some way. Maybe I had too. But I didn't really think so. I didn't feel changed. At least not in ways as obvious as some of the girls in my class. They ganged together more. And made a lot of business in annoying the older boys. They took their coats from the cloakroom and hid them over the back wall. They took their lunchboxes and put dirty pebbles and slimy banana skins into them. And then they got taken behind the lunch shelter and kissed by those boys.

The changed girls walked around like they owned the playground. Arm in arm, sometimes skipping forward in long lines. I was never part of the skipping. Or the kissing. At first I felt anger balling in my stomach and rolling up to my throat. My eyes prickled with bitterness when I saw them having a good time. Laughing privately and looking out from under their long hair at the older boys. They reminded me of the neighbours' cats that peeped out from behind the shrubbery whenever we passed. The girls left me to myself, and so mainly I played with the boys from my own class.

Three Goals In was my favourite, and I became good at it. At first I think whoever was in goal gave me an easier time because I was the only girl playing. But then I started shooting the ball past them, between legs, over shoulders. They'd never know how much I practised at home in the evenings. Whamming an old soccer ball against the garage door. I'd have Maeve stand there just so I could work at it. She looked terrified when it came close to her face or belly. Doing my best not to hurt my sister was how I learned to place the ball. And the boys in the class got me to join their teams when we played proper football. It was as if we were all figuring out a way to deal with the changed girls. I was ignored, and so too were the boys in my class. Forsaken for the older boys. They were confused, but of course nobody said anything about it. We were like people confronted with girls we'd known suddenly inhabited by aliens. I'd seen a film about something like this.

And now summer is nearly over in Adare and I'll be put among brand-new boys and girls. Well, not all new. Our cousin goes to the school. Paudge will be in the same class as me. I feel sure that he will walk around his school like a cruel little king. He already behaves like that in the house. And he will tell the classmates nasty stories about me and my family. And I'm worried that one of these stories will involve what happened in the bathroom not long after we got here.

Maeve didn't like the blue bedroom at first, but when we arranged our things around it and in the wardrobes and on the dressing table, it felt like being on holidays. Before Benny was born we had been to Butlin's Holiday Camp with our mother and father. We stayed in a room with two big beds. I loved the feeling of putting clothes out on the bed, slowly unpacking the bag belonging to Maeve and me. Things smelled nicer because it wasn't home. On the first day in Adare I tried to bring that feeling back, but Maeve started stuffing her clothes back into the bag and saying, *No no no,* until our father spoke to her in a low threatening voice. *We have to make the best of this for a while.* I whispered to her that we should pretend it was Butlin's. She looked at me full of suspicion. But then she pushed me aside to get at her clothes, and she went looking for a shelf to store them.

Our father put Benny's cot together.

Our mother took out his clothes, folded so small and square that they looked like bright handkerchiefs.

We found the bathroom that our aunt said was ours and ours only.

It was across the hall and it was tiled in a lovely sea-green colour. The tiles had raised designs on them and when I let my eyes slip out of focus they looked like waves tumbling down the walls. There was a narrow tall cabinet for towels and a round mirror with three bulbs over it. The bath was big, maybe twice as big as the bath in our old house. It was white and it looked clean enough to never have been used.

This was our bathroom, and seeing it was the first time since arriving in Adare that I felt pleased with something.

Sometimes I went in there to brush my hair, when I could've done so at the wide winged mirror at the bedroom dressing table. I took a long time with the brushstrokes. I liked to wash my hands with lemony soap pumped from a crockery bottle on the sink. I'd open the cabinet and smooth the towels, making sure that they were folded neatly. I'd have lived in the bathroom if there was a way.

Then came some trouble about the hot water. A thick hard red switch in the airing cupboard downstairs heated water for our bathroom and the other one, the bathroom as white as a fridge used by our aunt and uncle and cousins. Our aunt said something to our mother about the hot water and how they would have to work things out so that there was enough left. *Nothing worse than running a shower that's not going to get hot. What can you do then only jump out of your skin under it, or not bother at all.* At times I could forget that they were sisters, for our aunt spoke to our mother like a cross mother.

So one evening our mother decided that the practical thing to do would be share a bath. Me, Maeve, and her. *Girls' bath-time. C'mon, it'll be a bit of fun. The bath is big enough for ten of us.* We let her run the taps and we brought towels across the hall when it sounded like it was nearly full. She was already stepping in when we got there. I suppose it was the surprise of that that led me to forget the door. She was pink and already blotchy from the steam. The scar from where they'd taken Benny out through her stomach looked like a shut-tight mouth with white narrow lips. I'd only seen it once before, and that was when there were stitches criss-crossing her skin like black needly teeth. She had her hand to her front, where the light fluffy hair was.

And then she slid into the water and told us to *hurry on girls this water won't stay hot forever.* An iceberg of foam, dewberry-smelling, covered her breasts but I could feel them, slippery and bobbing against my back. I pulled Maeve to me like that, and we sat like people rowing a boat to some destination behind us. At first it was kind of embarrassing. Then I liked the sense of comfort: my mother soaping my back, me scrubbing Maeve's. Then we turned around, our legs knocking awkwardly against the sides of the bath, so that I could soap our mother's back. Maeve took a nailbrush to mine; I screamed and told her I'd drown her if she didn't put it down.

We took the plug out before we stood up. It was fun to feel the water rushing away either side of us, between our legs. And we all stood up at the same time, feeling strange and heavy-legged, and at the same time our cousins came in.

Before I knew that I had to get a towel, quick, towels for all of us, before I moved, I stared at them staring. Paudge looked like he had been shoved in the door by Stiofán, who lingered behind on the threshold. Eyeballing each one of us in turn. It's worse for our mother, I thought, it's much worse. With her hands clutched against the places they couldn't be permitted to see, but already had, she screamed at them to *get out GET OUT ye little bastards!* I stepped out to get the towels from where they sat in a cream and green pile on the closed toilet seat. The boys left. But I had seen that last look from Paudge: up and down his eyes ran, as if they were ants scurrying up my legs. As if his freckles were being flicked onto my skin. I slammed the door shut and, to make our mother laugh, I shoved my shoulder against it.

We dried off silently, bumping against each other between the bath and sink.

I knew that I wouldn't be allowed to forget this. They'd never dare to tease our mother. And Maeve was too young to bother; she always looked like she'd start crying at whatever one or other of them said to her. *Can you pass the butter? Where's my soccer ball?* Maeve saw every word from them as a threat. So I'd get the brunt of their jibing and joking about the bathroom. The thought of breakfast next morning made me feel sick. I felt like I'd never been soaped and cleaned in the bath at all. Paudge's dark eyes had dirtied everything.

It is his eyes that Maeve does not like. She decides this early on. They are brown, but not soft kind brown like Robin's. They are not eyes that dance with jokes, eyes that spill laughter out into the edges and crinkle it up. Paudge's eyes are blackish like windows at night-time. They are the same as his father's, but his father's seem to catch the light better and they flash like new coins sometimes. When Paudge looks at her she thinks that a deep well is calling her to look in and then fall down.

And ever since the bathroom he just stares and stares.

When Eva says, *Something to look at?*, angry and red, he thinks about it with his eyes, slowly blinking, and then says, *No, not yet.* Maeve sees her sister turn redder and she runs upstairs. The bathroom accident has made things even more strange in the house.

The willow tree protects them, though. It covers them when they bring dolls and books down there. When their mother starts to come there, it is as if she too has found out how to hide from Paudge's eyes. And Benny likes the shushing of the long leaves; it makes him take a sleep any time their mother brings him in.

Maeve thinks that under the tree they are like the group of children under the tall dame's skirt at Eva's school pantomime. The dame was a man teacher with his cheeks made red and lips too. He wagged his finger crossly as he walked tall on sticks, and his skirt was as wide as a car. It opened and boys and girls came skipping out. She really wanted to be one of them. Just at the part when they came out. After that, no, because she would not want to be on the stage dancing with everyone watching. So at the willow tree she plays at dancing out from under the dame's skirt.

She is left under there alone one afternoon. Eva must finish something for school that she is making from cardboard boxes; their mother is trying to feed Benny upstairs. He has been yowly and troublesome this past week. But Maeve has her dolls for company. And then she hears Paudge. And Stiofán. They are talking in low worried voices. Something has happened, something that they would prefer to hide. They talk as if they are trying to bury it with their quiet voices at the bottom of the garden. She has seen television programmes where someone is killed and then great trouble is taken to cover it up. The killed people are usually women. The killer person is usually a man. He gets discovered in the end, even if it is years later. She is not allowed to watch these programmes, but sometimes, especially if she sits on the floor between the armchair and the couch, she gets to see them. And now it feels like her cousins have done something dreadful. She cannot dare come out from under the willow.

And then she hears her sister's crying from inside the house. She must be in the kitchen, and not the bedroom where she had all her small boxes laid out, with glue and pieces of tinfoil. What has happened? Then their mother, shouting. *Jesus Christ. How did this happen?* The cousins stop talking suddenly. Like a knife has come down on the words passing between them. One of them, two of them, has done something. Maeve must go to the kitchen and discover what.

She builds herself up to burst through the willow leaves, to run so fast that her cousins will only see her for a second. Like the Road Runner, with his legs whirling in a white cloud of speed. Maeve runs.

In the kitchen her sister is lying on the bench that runs alongside the kitchen table. Her arms dangle down to the floor and Maeve is surprised at how long and stick-like they seem. Their mother holds her leg up and gently turns it. *How does this feel? How does this feel? Do you think your ankle might be broken?* Eva is white like chalk but her eyes are red from crying. She frightens Maeve. Maeve should go to hold her sister's hand but she cannot make her feet move to the bench.

Their mother must wait until their father comes home. There is nobody else in the house who can drive them to the doctor. And when Eva comes back very late that night she has been in the hospital for hours. Waiting. Their father's face is pulled out of shape with anger. *Everything's a fucking wait these days. A child with a broken leg has to wait. No wonder she fainted when they finally took a look at it.* Maeve steps softly down the stairs to see what is going on in the kitchen. She must see if her sister is still fainted. But no: Eva sits there with a big white solid leg next to her thin brown one. She drinks a cup of tea. Beside her on the table is a plate of chocolate biscuits. Their aunt and uncle are there too. Everyone has questions for Eva. She looks tired enough to be nearly dead. She says that she just wants to go to bed.

But when they are all in their blue bedroom Eva tells them what happened. She is lying back on two pillows. Maeve will let her sleep on the outside of the bed tonight, for sure, even though she herself hates sleeping next to the wall under the window. It makes her nervous. Trapped. Hands to the cold blue wall.

Eva tells them that she climbed onto the dressing table so that she could put her cardboard village on top of the wardrobe. She did not want anyone to sit on it accidentally. Or interfere with it. Maeve knew she meant the cousins: them, because of the way she said inter*fere*, flicking her eyes in the direction of the bedroom door. She had to pull herself up almost onto the flat top of the wardrobe so as to leave the village flat and safe there. She blew away some dust and pushed a shoebox out of the way.

Then the wardrobe started to shake. First she thought it was her doing, that she had not been careful to keep her balance. She turned around to try to find her feet, place them on the edge of the dressing table. Paudge was there, tilting the wardrobe by opening and wagging its heavy door. Eva says that she asked him to stop. But that he pulled it even further forward and that was when she fell. She dropped on her bent leg onto the dressing table and from there onto the floor. She says she felt a *horrible cracking sound*. Paudge was gone. She says she felt like milk, and then she dropped into sleep.

Their mother had to block herself against the door to stop their father rushing out to find Paudge and their aunt and uncle. She had to beg him not to *raise hell*. *Please*, she said, *not tonight. Let's just let Eva sleep*. She looked so tired, Maeve thought. Like her face was rubbed and rubbed until it was stretched and smeared. *We'll sort this out in the morning.* The last time she had seen her mother look so tired was when she had given Benny his first real milk from her nipples. She looked like he had drunk everything inside her.

Maeve hears her get up in the middle of the night. She knows it's their mother because the cot squeaks a little as she leans over to take Benny out. Maeve thinks this is different to the usual business: Benny always cries first, and then she takes him up. Now he whimpers a bit, because she has woken him. They leave through a slice of pale light from the landing.

Benny little manny my Benny my manny.

He knows his mother now. She is softness. She is a safe smell. When that smell wraps around him he knows he will get food and cleanness.

He bumps against her skin. Down a step, down a step, down a step. And then they are on flat ground.

He rocks with her. And hunger comes shivering through him.

He always has to cry for food but now she makes it happen without crying. The waft of cloth past him. She sets herself up for his mouth. It is dark where they are, and this feels different. There is more movement trying to find the place to drink. Her fingers wet his lips with warmth and then they press herself into his mouth.

He is drinking now and it feels richer and warmer than before. More and more, so much more that some of it slips out of his mouth.

But she is doing something else with her other hand.

She is holding something else.

He hears her voice. But it seems faraway. Just like he can hear it when she is somewhere else in the house. Faraway, but still there.

She is talking to someone who is not there.

Her voice is low and nice and soft and sad.

She talks.

Then stops.

Then talks.

He wonders about what is happening. But the drinking is so warm and comfortable he drops down a little. It is still going into his mouth, but slower now.

She talks. And stops.

And suddenly the drinking is over.

And they go up a step, up a step. His face on her shoulder. She rubs his back.

Before she lays him down she presses his face to hers. He tastes wet and warm on her face, but it is not as sweet as his feed.

After the page with the drawing of the red-roofed house, that house of my father's happiest time, the diary continues with a postcard. It's glued in, turned on its long side and taking up most of the page. The card shows a spread of smooth lake water between two pieces of land. It's tremendously blue, in that saturated postcard way, and it reminds me of those pictures of fjords in my geography schoolbook. There's no date in the margins. I wonder if the postcard has writing on its other side. But I can't detach it, so I move to the next page to look for more about the place.

His writing fills the lines, clutters them all the way past the margin on the outer edge. I'm startled to see this. Not just because there's so much writing. But because it reminds me of my own economical way with school copybooks. He taught us to make things last as long as possible.

August 1986

I am on the train from Boston to New York going past so many inlets and small marinas that everyone down this coast must own a boat. Or they spend a lot of time around people who own boats. This makes sense, because I have learnt that in America everyone tries to borrow someone else's holiday house. Or boat. At the politician's house in New Hampshire he told me and Robin that *the buzzards were circling*. I suppose we must have looked at him strangely, because he explained that he meant people would be keener than usual to come and stay at this lake house of his. Now that there were new floors down and the walls painted by us. All these boats along the shores of Rhode Island and Connecticut make me feel like I too might want to try my luck borrowing one. If I knew such a person who owned one. But still, there is something begging about that. The kind of cheeky attempt that makes people say, *Oh don't be so Irish*. I have never been quite sure what that meant, really, but I associate it with pulling a stroke or expecting more than your due.

I wonder if maybe I start to act like that then maybe I'll pick up more work and make more money sooner so that I can go back home to Belinda. Just before I left for the six months' work she told me that she was pregnant and that I was not allowed to stay longer in America than planned for fear the baby would arrive before I got back. I remember how she smoothed her hand over her belly when she said that. Her belly was still flat and it was hard to imagine it becoming round and taut. But it would and I would not see it do that. So I have to be sure to return when I said I would. I'm sure to have enough money by then. That money will be a deposit on a house. Not much will give me more pleasure than swooping down to take Belinda from her sister's house. That arrangement makes sense while I am away. Of course it does. We gave up our flat in Limerick city and she moved out to Adare. But I know that her sister does not see the wisdom in me going to America for six months to make money. Didn't I hear her saying it to her husband. *It's not all about money, ya know. He should tip along like he was doing and stay with his wife while she's carrying.* I remember her calling it *an exercise in greed. Quick money, oh quick money, that's what everyone wants.* She sounded like the nun she would have become if she had not defected from the convent. Fucking bitch, I thought. But if I had not overheard I would be better off, so I pretended nothing. And then I left.

This trip to New York has come at the end of a big

job on the politician's house outside Boston. Robin and myself work well together. I must say that we do. We have done so since meeting in the hostel and deciding to make a go of it. My first night in America and I was the oldest person in the hostel. Until I saw Robin standing thumbing through a newspaper. We hit it off – *senior citizens*, as he called us – and answered a *Wanted: Painters* ad. After that first job we have not been a day short of work and we are often working the full seven. And I suppose that would test even the best of working conditions. But Robin is always cheerful. Always. Jesus, sometimes it makes me want to throw a paint scraper at his whistling face. And good-looking, too. So he makes friends very easily wherever we are. I am one who hangs back, mostly. And women. He needn't spend one night alone if he doesn't feel like it. But because we sleep in the van to save money he doesn't bollix our situation by bringing women back. I am grateful to him for this. For never making a deal of things. He knows that I miss Belinda like hell. I showed him a photograph of us. One snapped at her friend's wedding. We had just come in from the dance floor where we jived and I swung her down between my legs. We look hot and definitely drunk. I told him it was pure hell to be without her. He laughed at the choice of words – pure hell – and then he got serious and said he could only imagine.

I am going to New York to get away from him so as to come back still liking him. And to give him a chance with the daughter of the politician. She is older than him and she showed up to check that everything was going according to plan. I knew she had it for him the minute she turned on her heel and whisked off down the path to her car. I knew because she turned around for a split second. Robin leaves that kind of impression. And she was on for it, and so was he. So all-round it was best to leave them to their own devices.

The motion of the train is soothing. Under you and surrounding you, but not the way an airplane makes you aware of its operations. I remember feeling sick when the plane to Boston left the ground at Shannon. Speed, more speed, hard top speed, and then your stomach scooped out when it lifts off. I would not have felt like this if I had not been on my own. Alone on the inside seat with plenty of time for thinking. It was not the first time I had been on a plane, but it put me wondering about what if it was the last. Of course this was mainly because I decided to read the safety instructions. In the event of. Cabin pressure. Masks. How you could take off the door and zip down along an inflatable slide. It made crashing into the ocean look like good fun at a holiday camp. There was even a picture of a woman in a knee-length skirt going down the slide. Her arms were projecting forward and she had probably taken her shoes off as the instructions asked. Once I got the possibility of a crash stuck in my head I decided that I wanted to be good at following these instructions. I imagined myself in the bracing position. Right hand over left. Head touching knees. Or the seat in front of you. When I got on this train to New York I looked around to see where the emergency exit window was and satisfied myself that I would be able to open it. In the event of. And soon we were running past such lovely inlets and meadows of fronds that a crash was the furthest thing I could imagine.

But just a while ago I saw something that I know will stay in my mind for a long time. Sometimes that happens, a thing being branded in there. I know I will think about

it for ages after because it was crazy-looking and also ...
I don't know ... comforting I suppose is what I want to
say. Out in the middle of the water there was a cabin. Just
that. Even in the couple of seconds I could see it before the
train pulled me away I saw that it had no land around it.
So it wasn't on an island. It was four walls and a door and
a window on a lake. I turned around in my seat to try and
keep it in my sight for just a bit longer. To be sure I had not
imagined it. The woman in the seat behind me seemed surprised and a bit nervous when my head popped up over the
seat. This reminded me of being on the school bus when
I was a boy. How we would persecute the girls by looking
down at them and saying stupid stuff. But the cabin was
already far behind me. I will sit on the right side of the train
coming back so as to see it again. It has put an idea in my
head. How I want to look after Belinda and our baby when
it arrives. I want to take them away somewhere the three
of us can live with nobody pestering us. With no family
wondering if we were stuck for money. With no sister or
parents looking in on things to see if there is enough food
in the fridge. Of course it will not be a place like the cabin
on the lake. But it could be somewhere near water. Or at
least where you could hear the sound of trees telling secrets
to each other, as I used to imagine them doing when I was
small. Birds. Then I would be happy and so would my wife
and my baby.

*I keep my eyes fixed on the end of the page for fear the garda will know that I'm
shaking. Reading my father's voice as this younger fella makes me feel like I'm
stomping all over the thoughts he found strong enough to write down. It makes me
feel like a sneaky little pryer. The very reason I never kept a diary myself. Fear of
exposure. Making myself naked to myself and anyone who'd sneak a read.*

I'm afraid to find out more. But I'm in there now, and I have been since the minute my hand felt out this diary at the back of the drawer. And much as I dread what might follow on these pages, I like the sound of his voice. Optimistic. And kind of shy at himself to be writing all this down. And the magical way he describes the cabin. It makes me want to have lived on that lapping water.

Barna, 1996

Tinsel and Holly

Christmas and New Year are over since two weeks ago but our father still wants to leave up the decorations. Maybe this is because he went to such trouble to buy so many of them, the green and red painted balls and the thick strands of tinsel, and then he made the others, spraying pine cones with silver and dabbing pretend snow onto the sharp teeth of the holly leaves. He was worse than Maeve for wanting to leave them around the place. But they bothered me. Leaving up the decorations is like hanging onto something that is gone, gone, gone. As if you would try to make your birthday last for a whole month. It gives me a lonesome feeling, this hanging on. I even offered to do all the work of taking them down and putting them into boxes. But no, they are still here. Even the lights. They twinkle in the evening and make our small house look like a happy cosy place from the outside. A place having a party every single night.

I like where we are now. There are no people next to us; we

are the only people at the end of a little road. We have to walk to the end of our road and then onto the main road before seeing another house.

And my school is alright, too. After the accident in Adare that broke my ankle and split all its bones into pieces my father would not have us living there any more. I wonder if Paudge still thinks about all the trouble he got into. I wonder what he would think if he knew that I have a limp now. And that I probably will have it forever. His fault. But I don't hate him. Maybe I would if the boys and girls at the school were mean about it. They're not, so far, anyway. Sometimes I see the girls' faces working like they are doing division or spellings in their heads, and it makes me think that they might be inventing mean things to say. Every day I go there I wait for their mouths to twist and burst out with those things. When the Christmas holidays arrived I had a long time off from expecting them to turn. It felt nice to wake up in the morning and instead think about how many television programmes we would be allowed to watch and how many bars might be left in the selection box. And now I'm back at school and the girls have not turned. Yet.

But maybe if they could see the silly decorations hanging around our house they would. It would be a good excuse to make up stories about my family. Some people like to do that. At the house in Adare I heard our aunt making a speech to our mother about what she thought of our family. Much more so our father.

It was the night he announced that he had found a house to rent near the sea in Barna. *Barna,* I thought. *That's like a nice old woman's name.* Not only that, but he had a job driving a fish lorry into Galway to the city's restaurants. He looked so pleased with himself, and this made his words come out high and loud. Like the boy in my class whose voice gets stronger the closer he gets to spelling twenty out of twenty words in Irish. Our teacher has us spell them out loud because then we pronounce them at the end of each one. I imagined our father spelling *f-i-s-h FISH* and *r-e-s-t-a-u-r-a-n-t RESTAURANT* to show his pride to our aunt who sat with her hands tightly holding a mug of tea. Something was about to burst out, I felt sure, when she put the mug down so slowly and quietly that it didn't make a sound on the coaster. It was as if the mug and coaster were made of exactly nothing instead of pottery and glass.

Our mother was looking nervously from our father to aunt, aunt to father. I was told to go out to the front room with Maeve and Benny. Which I did. Leaving Benny on Maeve's lap and turning on the television for them. I went back to the kitchen. My damaged ankle made me walk slowly and carefully anyway, all the time stepping like there was something tender and precious under my foot. I used to take extra care by pretending Benny's little hands were all over the ground and walking heavily on any of them would make him cry. So it was easy to get back to the crack in the door without them hearing me. I was proud of my cleverness in not closing the door fully behind me when I left with Maeve and Benny.

She talked with a sharp oily voice.

She said our father and mother were *freeloaders*.

Our mother had *never been like that*, she said, but our father had made her *part of his scamming*.

She called him *arrogant* and *prideful* and said that he should be ashamed of himself, for *someone without twenty pounds in the bank*, she would guess.

And he would *drag the children down with him*.

Her speech was long and you would think that there was nobody at all in there with her. That's how quiet everyone else was. Our uncle had a trick of being in a room and sitting as if he belonged to the table and chairs, so it was no surprise that I didn't hear him. Anyway, he was too afraid of her to even think of trying to calm her down. She bossed him around like a bold dog. Our mother was her sister, and I had never heard her say a vexed or angry word to her. Our father. Then he started. His voice was low and his words marched like quiet frightening steps in a scary film. I couldn't hear everything.

... the most insulting ...
... jealousy must be a desperate ...
... always the ones with ...

If he had been a teacher I would have been crying just at the way the words fell like cold rain down on my head.

Then a chair was suddenly scraped on the tiles and I had to move back into the hall. Going backwards on the bad ankle was treacherous. Pain zoomed up my leg and I nearly shouted. I found Maeve staring at naked people on the television and I wanted to see them too but Benny was free on the couch and inching on his belly like a worm.

Two days after that, on a Sunday morning, we brought all our things from the blue room and the green bathroom to another house. Our father had the loan of the fish van. There was no name on the side of it and it was an old old white colour. Benny sat in front on our mother's lap, Maeve and me in the back with the stuff. Our father said that it *might smell a bit off* and it did. So off that I could not think of a line of bad smells to which it belonged. And it was dark because there was no window into the driver's part, like in Robin's van. When we went around corners it felt like we were being rolled around in a can. When it picked up speed it seemed a lot more frightening than it would have been if we could have seen the road. Maeve went completely silent after a while and I imagined her face as deadly white. I did things like flexing my fingers and toes, pressing my feet against boxes, rooting around for our dolls.

When we got to our new place and the door was opened at the back of the van, the smell of fish spilled out and the sea raced in on top of us. We were near the shore. It felt cold and healthy. I wanted to hug my arms around myself and run on the spot. *This is the best place ever,* I thought. *I can't wait to go exploring.* There was no time that evening; we brought in boxes and tried to fix bedrooms for ourselves. Maeve and I would share one, and Benny would sleep in our parents' room. The house was small but I loved it like it was a cottage I had made for our dolls.

It looks even more like a cottage now, with the Christmas lights twitching pink and green inside the front window. On the dark lawn I push a bit of snow together with my feet. There isn't much snow, nowhere near enough to think about a snowman. I step back toward the front fence. I hear the sea talking to itself behind me. Our house is like one of those houses where talking animals live in stories. Tomorrow, I hope. Tomorrow will be the day for turning it back to normal walls and windows, for filling a box with tinsel that looks like crispy silver and golden hair. Our father will have grown tired of them. They won't be a magic game to him any more.

I think about when he gets giddy with happiness. About some new book or game for us. Or something he says he has invented and how nobody has thought of this before and how it could make him rich and famous. He used not be like this when we lived in Adare, no way, and I don't remember it before that either. Being in Barna seems to have changed him. His words and ideas flit around like butterflies. He reads things to us from his own books.

Come on, girls, girls, *now listen to this. The man who invented the submarine came from County Clare. John Holland. We went to school in the same town. Ennistymon. Can you believe it.*

I know, because I was photographed in a kitchen with an old woman, that I went to Ennistymon once. It was to meet my grandmother there. But she died when I was two and then there was nobody there for us to make the journey.

Our father turns the book to show us a picture of John Holland. He has a huge moustache and he is sticking out of what looks like a chimney with a big beak on it. You can't see below his ribs. He could be a midget for all we know. But he was famous. Our father reads in a very serious voice. *John Holland died in poverty. His work only achieved recognition many years later.*

Drag us down with him.

I wonder why our aunt was so angry.

I close my eyes. The sea seems to get louder when I do, the same as television.

I picture us all at the bottom.

As if our father had grasped our mother's hand and she took mine and I held Maeve's and Maeve stuffed Benny under her arm. And then we all followed his lead to the seabed. But we weren't dead. We just walked around doing the same things.

Maeve stands for a photograph next to a pile of seaweed. Her father indicates that she should step up onto it. She doesn't want to. It already smells vinegary and she is sure that walking on it will only release more of the smell. Just like stepping into cow dung as she did on the roadside in Adare with Eva and her cousins. That wasn't an accident; the boys pushed her into it. The crust on top cracked and one of her shoes was sucked into sticky green. She is so glad that they are gone from that house and those cousins. So glad that she could sing a song. So she climbs up along the pile of seaweed and throws her arms out for the photograph. It crackles like crisps under her feet. She doesn't like the look of it, those lumps like covered eyes all along the strands. But she is out on a walk with her father and it feels like the return of good times. She smiles without even being told to.

They have a bag of holly with them and they are not sure what to do with it. This morning her father took down the decorations at last. Eva rushed around to help. In a short time the living room looked boring and a bit cold. Eva said it looked like the walls at school when the teacher took down all the big pictures drawn for Christmas. Maeve sneaked the baby Jesus out of the crib and showed him to Benny. *Lookit, a baby like you.* Benny stretched out his hands and brought the baby's head to his mouth. Maeve grabbed it back just in time. Then the crib was put in a box and tinsel piled on top of it. Her father said that he would find a place to throw away the holly.

But it's still sitting behind them at the beach. They're sitting down too, to have a piece of chocolate. *And think about the world.* Her father's description for what they are doing, which is looking far out to sea. Maeve tries to see farther than just that blurred line where the sea and the sky meet. She feels sure that there must be something out there sailing near that line. Or maybe there are things travelling under the sea, and so she has no hope of seeing them. Eva had laughed at their father's man in the submarine. *He looks like an eejit with that moustache.* But Maeve thought his idea was great. In a submarine you would get to see starfish and all the things that lived secretly on the bottom. And travelling could be secret, too. You could run away and arrive in another country. All done quietly under the waves.

She is glad that they live near the sea now. It makes everything bigger, even if their house is fairly small. Of course, nothing could be as cramped as the blue room in Adare. For a few nights it had been cosy, being tucked up with Eva and hearing their mother and father whispering in the other bed. But then Eva started kicking and Benny would cry at all sorts of hours. And their father had to stop their mother crying by making silly loud kissing sounds. Maeve was so afraid of Paudge that sometimes her stomach tightened enough to be sick, and she didn't like their aunt's voice, and the phone had a silly annoying noise. Instead of *brinnngggg-brinnngggg* like in their old house it rang like a toy. *Meeeepppp-meeeepppp.* She wanted to put a cushion over it. That was the way to smother things; she saw a man doing it to a woman on television.

Yes. It was nice to be in Barna.

Bar-na.

It means gap. Her father picks up a fist of seaweed and starts trying to plait it like hair. It crunches thickly in his hands. *It's the Irish word for gap.* Even though she is still keeping her eyes skinned for ships she knows that he is smiling. Information about words and descriptions of things always seem to make him happy. *I like the idea. I like the notion of us living in a gap. D'you know.* Maeve didn't, but she said nothing. *We are that kind of family. Not interested in fitting into. Into the mainstream way that everyone else lives.* He is talking a lot on today's walk, and they still have the holly to look after. She listens closely and deeply to what he says. For she knows that she won't understand it all right now. Not when he talks in this distant way. Like he is sending his words all the way out to that edge along the sea. She will line up his words for herself later and maybe some things will make sense. *No, I'll tell you. I'll tell you this. If I had my way I would have us living on an island. Or in the heart of a forest.*

She knows that he talks a lot about *we* and *us* and *family* lately. Those words happen more often than they used to. Maeve wonders if living near the sea has something to do with this. If it makes you want to run along sand and splash in the water, if it makes you feel this happy and shiny, then maybe it makes you talk about different things, too. She stands up and turns round to the holly bag. It looks like cats' claws are trying to poke through it. *Alright Maeveen, let's get rid of the last of the Christmas.*

Laughing and laughing and laughing.

It runs from her chest into Benny's, it jumps him up and down.

96

She is talking again to someone who is not there. At least, he cannot see someone's shape. He likes being held when she laughs like this. It makes him feel like laughing too, and he does, and then she is laughing at that and at the someone who is not there.

Benny feels comfortable in this room and the other one. He likes being bathed and he knows the shape of the tree outside the window. And his sisters have a happy time too. They talk to him more and they lift him up and down and he does not feel like he is going to fall down any more.

Then his mother is quiet. The laughing talk is over.

She presses him to her neck. It feels warm there. Warmer than before. But Benny feels frightened. He wants to move his head back but she presses it there. His mother's skin feels too warm. It even smells a bit different.

He feels her hand leave the back of his head. She brings it to her own head, to the front. She sits back suddenly and his knees knock against her. He is still tight to her. Even though he is tight to her she feels loose and soft.

She talks to herself. Benny wants the others to come in and see if something is the matter. The way that they do when he is uncomfortable in his blanket. Sometimes he does not even have to cry. Someone just knows and comes in.

He wants that now as his mother's hands loosen from around him and he slides down into her lap. Is she asleep? He does not know. And he cannot move from where he is. His fingers hold onto the buttons on her dress. He tries to pull on them to make her notice.

He hopes that someone will come in.

The Shed

The new big plan is to build a shed. Our father says that he and Robin will put it up in one day. *One day, tops.* He smiles that wide clowny smile: the one given to plans for making things, inventing games for us, or something in a book about scientific discoveries. The smile with big shiny eyes for big new plans. Our mother nods her head gently. At first I think that she doesn't believe in his plan for this magic one-day shed. But when I look for a longer time I see that she is tired. Ready to fall asleep at the table. Her eyes are low and I notice how long her eyelashes are. Long enough to sweep shadows on her cheeks. I would like her to have a nice bath and then go to bed, but Benny is vexed and red and he cries from between clamped jaws. She holds him over her shoulder and rubs him to quietness. It takes a long time. Benny is very agitated these days. He seems to always want to be soothed.

And Robin. We haven't seen him since the day he helped us bring the house stuff to Adare. Hearing on Sunday night that he will come on Saturday makes happiness stack inside me like firewood that I think might be enough to last all the way through the week.

Now that one of the girls in my class has starting saying things, Robin's face coming to smile in my mind just before I fall asleep feels even better. He doesn't know about my limp and how the cousin caused it. But I know he will be kind about it. That's just his way. His face will first look puzzled and then crossness will spread over it like clouds. Just as it did the time someone took my bicycle from outside the house in Galway not long before we left for Adare. He might even call Paudge *a proper evil little bollix*, like the person we imagined must have taken the orange bicycle. I loved how he said it, the *rs* in *proper* like something ripping through the word and all the *ls* bubbling like hot oil. Sometimes Robin could turn words into cartoons like Tom and Jerry. I hope he will have something nasty to make of Paudge.

The girl in my class almost can't help herself, I think, when it comes to my leg. I feel like she was picked to be the speaker of the others' meanness. I saw her face tightening just before she said the first *So what happened to your leg, like?* Trying to chew the words back into her mouth, but of course they came out. And once they did, that starts it.

Were you in the war or something?

I saw a man on the bus to Galway with one huge shoe and another normal one.

Can you have an operation to fix that?

The girls dig at me more than the boys do. Nothing new about that.

I wonder if I had an older brother would he make such nasty jokes about me that I could handle anything at school afterwards. But brothers can really hurt you; I learned this from Ailbhe. She would come in crying because hers had put toffee in her hair or called her a *little bitch*. A older brother and a limp would be a bad, bad combination.

Around at home I never have to think about it. The lift and half-drag of my leg: I am used to this movement by now. The only time I feel aware of it is when I am down on the strand and it scuffs up more sand than usual and I can see my own trail behind me. Strange-looking, like a small animal burrowed along beside my good leg. The sight of it is proof of the limp that mostly I don't notice.

A man at the house closest to ours, the butter-yellow one on the main road, has a hole in his throat. We met him for the first time down at the strand with our father. His voice was a wheezy squeak and I suppose because he did not expect to bump into anyone he had left his shirt collar open. I tugged on the back of Maeve's cardigan when I saw her staring. The hole had a plastic piece around it that looked like a small porthole. I noticed that it was the same colour as his house. I wanted to look deeper but did not want to be caught. I know what he would feel: hot under the staring, anxious to cover up even though it was too late. Our father explained it to us when the man was far enough away not to hear. He spoke seriously and slowly. He traced a line down his neck and drew a circle; it was like he had chalk and a blackboard. *Ugh that's horrible.* Maeve tickled the knob on her throat. Like she was making sure it was good and strong and in no danger of being cut out. Our father told us that it was one of *several good reasons not to ever smoke.*

But I am happy that that man is down the road. His situation is worse, I know, but he knows what it is like to stick out. To have people turn and look. To look sorry for him.

Robin won't be like that when he comes to help with the shed.

I think about him at important times during the week.

Before the spelling test on Friday.

After my favourite dinner on Thursday: fish and chips.

And I walk back and forth in the kitchen to practise for the first time Robin will see me pull my leg. I don't want it to be too obvious. I make quick steps, as light as I can. Until it looks like I'm about to set off dancing. And then it just looks silly, so I stop.

Mostly I can forget the way he buttoned our mother's blouse that time when he gave the months of money. Not really forget, but head it off when it tries to come into my mind like a full and living picture. There was something so soft and secret about it that just remembering it for a second seems to make my eyes buzz dangerously. Our father read a book about mind-reading some time back. It wasn't just about mind-reading; it had things like hypnotism and suggestion and mesmerism and words that sounded nice but you knew that made them all the more menacing. He told us about convincing people to get on airplanes. *It's all about seeing into their fears. Seeing them better than they can see them themselves.* When Robin's fingers and our mother's buttons flashed in my head it seemed as clear as if it was happening there at the table, so alive that our father could surely tell what I was thinking. But he went on pouring milk into the cereal bowls. Stirring Maeve's to release the chocolate into the milk just as she liked it. He went on doing his things.

And soon he will build a shed with Robin's help, and he won't have a clue about what I know.

I wonder which would make the worse trouble: the money or the buttons.

Maeve walks around the shed that lies flat to the ground at the back of the house. Straight line, straight line, then crossways up to the point. Robin tells her that this is the apex of the roof and he directs her eyes to the top of the gable of their house. To show her what this means. Then she looks down at the wood triangle between her feet and finds it perplexing to imagine how it will become what Robin points at.

She stands on tiptoes and closes her eyes. Ballerina ballerina turn all around. Ballerina ballerina at the top of the house. She twirls and again and then topples. Her father shoos her back from the timber laid all over the grass. It's a steamrolled shed, she thinks, like the flattened kennel and cat she saw on a cartoon. How will it ever be brought to life and turned into a shed?

But it does, at some time between Maeve getting bored and hungry and watching television and then going back outside. Eva is walking through a doorway. Robin is nailing something with short taps of a hammer. Her father is turning down the edges of the black gritty stuff that will make a roof. He curses as it doesn't do what his hands want. It's a shed alright. But it looks too lovely to fill with stuff. She would love to have it as a playhouse. It would be perfect: the small table and chairs, the television that Eva made for them from a cardboard box with bottle caps for knobs and a picture of mountains and a lake stuck on. At first Maeve thought this was great. So clever. Real-looking. Then she realized that the picture got boring. And anyway you didn't watch a programme about mountains and a lake, at least not a children's one. But because Eva had made it she started to like it again just for what it was: a humpy line of blacky-green mountains and a lake that looked like it would be cool and delicious to jump into in summer. And her father had given it a bit of magic by drawing a tiny house floating on the lake. He winked at her behind Eva's back and sketched the house with a pencil. Because it was small and made from faint grey lines it looked like a ghostly house gliding on the blue glass of the lake. Eva passed by the television box and didn't notice. Then she passed again and looked back over her shoulder. Stopped. Walked to it slowly. As if it was something much stranger than a penciled house. When she guessed that their father had done it, she started laughing. Then their mother saw it and said it was very clever. *Like something from a travel programme.* Maeve was surprised by how serious their father's voice was when he said it was his dream house. *If I had my way we'd all live in a kind of island house like this.* They all looked at him because he spoke so so carefully. They expected him to start laughing, letting them know he was joking. But he didn't. Their mother said that she wanted them all to live in a yellow submarine, and she went out to the kitchen humming *yel-low sub-mar-ine ... yel-low sub-mar-ine.*

But she sees that the shed has no windows. So it wouldn't be very nice for a playhouse. She walks around to see if there's one at the back. The wall is blank. The shed is blind. If she went in there now and shut the door it would be as dark as the cupboard under the stairs at her aunt's house. She ran in there once to escape from Paudge who was chasing her with nettles he had grasped in a plastic bag. And that is where she found her mother. Was she hiding too? Maeve was not sure why she would be in there, sitting against the rack of shoes. She put her finger to her mouth and drew Maeve to sit between her knees. Maeve remembers that they said nothing, not even a whisper. The air was thick and dark. They breathed together, then apart, then together again. Her mother smelled of chocolate and Benny's milky drool. Maeve liked this secret of theirs, sitting in the dark under the stairs while the house moved around them.

When Maeve comes back around to the front of the shed, she sees her mother take her father's hand and they go into the shed. *For a quiet kiss,* Robin says to Eva and her. *Kess.* He says it loudly and it sounds wet, like a kiss. *Come outta there and don't be sneakin' kesses behind your children's backs.* Robin holds Benny, sort of loosely-looking, but totally safely at the same time. If anyone could build an island house and push it out into the middle of a lake, it would be Robin. It would suit him. He was an entirely alone person. He would probably be happy out there. Robin brought happiness with him where he went. Like a present. Today he helped to build a shed and he had their father talking in the voice that Maeve thought he left behind at their old house with the red roof. Robin made their mother and Eva laugh. Separately and together. He had Maeve hold Benny and then he picked up both of them and pretended to drop them over the back wall.

At the end of this Saturday Maeve wonders if all the laughing means that they are quieter for more of the time than they think. That they are afraid of the next move to another house. And what might make it happen.

But the shed. The shed must mean that they will be in this house for a while. It stands there, even more orange because the sun is going down. Like there is a fire warming it from the inside.

Later Maeve takes out the television box and thinks about colouring the island house with her orange crayon. It might look like a house on fire on a lake. Maybe such a fire would only last for a minute. Or maybe it would burn on for ages. It was one of those questions that her father could look up in one of the encyclopaedias he bought when the library in the city was selling old books.

Instead of waking her, this night he is woken. Her hand under his back wiggles him up and away.

They move through the dark house. She does not turn on a light. She holds him with one arm and moves the other in front to steer them. The door squeaks. Coldness pours round them.

Then they are outside. It feels louder than the house, but not with sharp sounds. A huge quietness surrounds them. He feels it press into his ears and eyes. Then somewhere behind his head there is a long whisper. *Shsssssh.* It stops. And comes again. It is not a person. It is something much bigger than that kind of voice. He feels very afraid and he shrinks as small as he can in her arms. Her feet crunch under them.

Another door sound. Then they are inside somewhere. There is a sharp smell. It is not a bad smell. Salty and a bit sweet. Like the bench where they go sometimes. Her feet sound different. They tap softly as she walks him around. She lowers down, sits and turns him to her. But he cannot see her. She rests him on her knees and takes his hands and presses them to her head. Her hands are cold but her head feels warm. He pats and pats and she seems to like that. She laughs.

Benny, I think you might be the only one in this house who knows me.

They stay there for what must be a long time. So long that he falls into sleep. He only wakes at the sound of the door closing behind them, then the long whisper, and then the path through the house that has stayed silent in sleep while they were gone somewhere else.

I read that I am born.

My heart pinches. It's so sharp and strange to see his account of it.

1 December 1986

She is here.

She is here.

Eva.

We have had her name ready for a long time. From when Belinda sent me a letter in Boston with this name written in capital letters in the middle of the page and lots of empty space around it. Eva. A name in its own right. Just like she might grow up to be a law unto herself. Belinda was very happy with this name. And even if I had not been, the way she presented it did not give me any choice. But I liked it. Eva. It floated alone there in the middle of the blue page. Like the tiny baby inside Belinda. Alone, but not alone.

Beautiful, beautiful Eva.

She is ours and she is her own. When I looked down into her eyes I knew she could not see me. And that made her even more her own person. Tucked away inside her eyes. The wary deep colour of seals' eyes.

What is she? She is mine. But I am having a hard time believing it.

I am writing this back at the house in Newcastle. They are over in the hospital for the night, maybe two nights. Belinda had to have a lot of stitches and she is in a lot of pain. But so happy.

I found this house for us. I bought it so we could live here and be our own world. Looking around it now I know that I must turn it inside-out and make it better for when they come back from the hospital. If I had enough time tonight I would paint all the rooms in soft summery colours. Like Neapolitan ice-cream. It belonged to a solicitor and it is painted in beiges and browns. Avocado in the bathroom. Makes my skin look sick in the mirror. I wish I had paint cards to look at, nice pale pinks and yellows, and vanilla white for the kitchen.

But I won't have time to do this for a while. I have to make sure I can get jobs lined up and bring in money. There are three coming up. Each should last two months. All of them flooring and fixing up rich people's houses out in Taylor's Hill and Knocknacarra. Fuckers trying to increase the value of their houses by adding a conservatory or a sixth bedroom. But they will take me close to summer. And when the weather warms up I can take on more outside jobs.

I have to think long-term now. This makes me feel safe. Because I know what I have to do and there can't be any dragging my heels when there is a house and a wife and a baby dependent on me. But I know that sometimes it will feel like a big wall about to fall down on me. The weight of it. I know that feeling. From just before I married Belinda. And again in Boston when I thought I would not get work and I would go home in debt.

Drinking by myself here at the kitchen table makes me feel things closely. But that is also because I am writing in this diary. With writing you could go too deep, like blades opening fletches of skin.

If I had a brother he would be holding me up in a bar and telling everyone assembled that I was a new father. A new father. I like how a new baby turns someone into something else. Something new. A baby has no choice. It arrives brand new. But it gives the rest of us a chance to make things over.

If I had a sister she would probably be clucking around and packing up her own baby stuff for Belinda.

I'll tip myself just one more finger of whiskey and raise it to my mother and father. Who would have loved to see this day. Good luck to them. Godspeed.

I am a man with a daughter. Which makes me a man in the world.

Robin would be a good one to ring now. I know he is somewhere on the Connemara coast. No interest in going back to Edinburgh so he said he would return with me and poke around for work here.

Another finger. Even if it is cheap stuff. The blaze of it makes me feel full of the most important thoughts in the world. Intentions. True things I can write down and hold myself to account for. I should ring Robin at the hotel he is building.

I am a father.

Saying it in my head first makes it stronger than the words on this page.

I am a father and I will be good and protective and a fighter for the best things for my daughter.

Goodnight little Eva.

And after I am born so are Maeve and Benny.

The diary has nothing between these events. To read it makes all our arrivals seem to happen in the same week, apart from the dates, and the handwriting that changes only a little. Poor Maeve doesn't get as much writing as I did. I scan the amount of writing about Benny. Also more than Maeve. But that's because I was the first and he was the boy.

But as I read on I see that Maeve has a different history, and that's because of her name. And the secret of it shocks me.

12 September 1990

I have another daughter.

This makes me ask myself how good I have been to my first. Eva is almost four. We have lived in Newcastle for the same length of time. How does a man measure whether he has made a good family or not? Eva cried when she would have normally done as a baby. She bypassed crawling and started walking from the shaky standing position she used to take against the couch. And she did not wait for us to be her audience. Belinda and I were putting up a shelf in the corner. We turned around to see her tottering. Not to us, as I thought all babies did. She moved toward some invisible thing, with her arms out and a wide smile. Eva was a good baby and a good child and I suppose that means we did our best for her.

She liked the green and especially the swing. I liked how it felt to push her. A split second of sending her off into empty space. My stomach gave a little twinge.

Now she has a sister.

Maeve. This time I asked for the name.

After the little sister I had. I never told this to Belinda. So it will not upset her and have her think our baby might be marked with bad luck. My sister's misfortune. She only lived for half a year. I was six or seven. I think now that I don't remember her at all. But it's not hard to conjure her up. Because she was a baby, and babies look the same. My mother and father were so happy that she was on the way after such a long time of being just the three of us. Of course, they did not know then whether it was to be a boy or a girl. To me it must have been like waiting for Christmas. And then she was here. And then she was gone. Crying in the kitchen. First baby Maeve. She drank milk and she slept and she cried tiny cries. Like a kitten. And then the awful howling of my mother. It terrified me. Cries that could tear a person in half. And my mother was such a small woman. My sister had died in her sleep. My mother's cries lulled but they never really stopped. I used to find her holding Maeve's clothes. Pressing her face into them. One time she rammed a tiny white cardigan into her pocket as if it was a handkerchief she had been caught blowing her nose on.

I will never tell Belinda or Maeve or anyone about my sister that left my life. When she was gone I felt a cold hollow in my chest. I had promised to myself that I would look after her forever. But I was not able to prevent whatever came and stopped her breathing in the cot that night.

So I must protect my daughter Maeve. I want her to have the name. I want to be able to say it out loud again. Call her with it and make up songs for sleep with her name in them. I will stay awake beside her every night.

Tea has been spilled on the corner of the page where Benny is born. Ragged brown eating into white. It reminds me of how he showed us the way to make an ancient map for buried treasure. Maeve squeezed the wet teabags between her hands to get the last thick brown drops. We laid the page into the muddy water in the bathroom sink. It had a skull and crossbones above an island that we made by tracing a map of Ireland. He found this very funny, especially where we marked the spot. Cavan, it looks like! You wouldn't find any doubloons up in that godforsaken spot! *And then he got annoyed because our details didn't match up as well to his. The ageing of the map had taken a full teapot and then all that time letting it cool. Gently lowering the map into it, but even more carefully taking it out so as not to tear the soft wet paper.* Jesus, girls. Ye might have at least buried it out on one of the islands. Achill, for example. Although that's not strictly an island, so … *And here is Benny's birthday dated like a much older time. A time when exciting things happened, like treasure and pirates fighting with cutlasses.*

1 October 1994

I am still laughing at the card Robin sent. IT'S A BOY! is written in round blue letters. You would wonder who comes up with ideas for these cards. A right racket. As if you need a card to make sure you know whether it is a girl or a boy. What happens when there are twins or triplets, though? I am sure I have never seen one. Belinda thought it was hilarious when I bought a card along with flowers to her. At least my card said, 'Welcome to the World, Little One.' That was the extent of my silliness. That and giving ten pounds to a woman begging with a child near the hospital gate. Sometimes I think becoming a father has made me a real soft touch. Belinda liked the flowers. Big yellow things. Flowers that looked like they might reach forward and swallow you into their fuzzy brown centres. And the girls brought a teddy bear for their new brother. They are thrilled to have him.

When we came home Maeve said that she liked the name. Benny. I suppose it is easier for a four-year-old to say. And now I can't remember which of us thought it up. I feel like we had been talking to him as Benny before we realized that we had named him. Well, at least that made things simpler. Better than if Belinda wanted to name him after her father. Ignatius would be a real cross of a name to bear. And Iggy is, I think, an insufferable name for a boy and man. There was an Iggy in my class at school. Just saying the name made you think you were mocking him. It sounded like something stammered. But Benny is a good name and it will fit both a boy and a man I think.

Belinda said that her crowd are coming down tomorrow. So I will let them have their visit and then arrive later to collect her. I am determined to avoid them if possible. They still look at me as if I

The bottom of the page is buckled and the ink at the end has bled and blurred the words. I'd like to know what words he used for how he thought my grandparents saw him.

I have a fair idea. But it would be good to know how what real words he put on it all the way back then. I only started to pay attention at the time Maeve cried beside me in the back of the car and I didn't mind that she picked up a sheaf of my white Communion dress to wipe her face.

Grandparents and Presents

They were at my First Holy Communion last year. But I haven't seen them since that morning outside the church in Adare. And now they're coming to Barna for our mother's birthday.

I know that this isn't wanted by our father because I hear him telling her. *You know that nothing good ever comes of us meeting. You know that. Nothing good whatsoever. I thought you knew that.* That high voice, the one like a teacher repeating the important things, the things that will be tested later on.

I wasn't sure why our mother had decided to celebrate her birthday as if she was a child. By this I mean, why she was having extra people to the house, why she was even having a cake when last year she decided to ban it. *No cake for my birthday this year. I don't like a fuss being made of it. Now, when I reach forty, I'll either want to vanish somewhere and hide from it or I'll want the biggest party known to creation.*

One of those odd times when I was made to think about how

our parents, my mother especially, thought about themselves.

Around that time too I saw her bringing her face close to her mirror, as close as if she was going to kiss the reflection, then holding the milky-blue skin round her eyes stretched between her finger and thumb. It made her eye bulge big and wet like the picture of that awful man in my book of *Tales of Poe*. In the mirror she saw me watching her and said that *any day now* she would look like a much older woman. *The television ads make it look like it's something that happens overnight and that you can fix overnight. But it isn't.*

She moved back from the mirror and tilted her head sideways and chin-up; she stroked her neck with both hands. This movement made her voice come out warbly. And that made her words sound even sadder. *It grows on you and you don't notice it until one day you step aside for a woman in Dunnes Stores and you realize that it's you in the mirror and you were thinking that woman's frowning too much.*

I suppose that my face showed that I was confused and didn't know if I should say something, or even if I was meant to be listening. For she was talking to me like she'd never done before. Like I was a sister or a friend. The way women on television programmes talk to each other. Sharing problems and worries, passing them back and forth over cups of coffee, widening their eyes with each new dreadful piece of the story. But then she jerked her head back from the mirror as though her hands in the glass had tried to reach out and grab her throat. Like the evil reflection of Snow White's mother. *Silly talk. Nonsensical talk.* Her voice went back to the normal one she used for me. *Now, if I could get control of these headaches then maybe I wouldn't frown so much, isn't that the case?*

On this morning of her birthday she looks exactly the same as she did last year. But I wonder if she saw something new in the mirror that made her think those same thoughts about getting old. Some tiny thing that made her believe that her whole face would eventually crack like dried mud. Still, she looks excited when we come piling on top of her bed with the presents that our father took us to buy. Maeve gives her a new hairbrush and insists on drawing it through her hair before our mother even has a chance to take it in her hand. I give her lipstick and eyeshadow that I bought in the same chemist as the hairbrush. It took a while to find what I thought might be good colours. Our father left us to ourselves in there, and when the chemist lady saw me going through the rack of little boxes she came over and asked about our mother's eyes and pointed to some that would be *suitable and flattering for green eyes.* These boxes had squares of orange and brown. I wanted to tell her that I needed something much more: colours that would make her eyes look bright and shiny as a tiger's. I'd seen them in a magazine. The woman's face was different, but her eyes were like our mother's, and she wore big dashes of pink and purple. And a thick line of black along the top. If I'd seen that, surely I could get it, and it would work. But the chemist lady seemed very sure, nodding in a way that made you notice the big roll of flesh between her chin and her white collar. *Yes,* that fat nod said, *trust me. I'm rarely wrong.* The lipstick was easier and I let her roll six or seven pinks and reds on my hand. I went for the reddest. It looked classy. And I could tell that the chemist lady didn't like it as much. But I had to get the better of her on something.

I felt like we could have stayed all afternoon in that chemist, it smelled so sweet and crispy-clean. Like vanilla and new white paper and Benny's colic medicine. There were lots of older people in there, women mainly, and they sat down waiting for things from behind the counter. I wondered if our grandmother would look much different from when she and our grandfather turned up at the Communion. Turned up, because nobody was expecting them. Or most likely our mother knew, and that was sort of a surprise for me. Except it didn't feel too much like a happy surprise when I saw our father's face in the church porch. And that when they walked so nervously towards me and Maeve I felt sorry for them and how long it had been. I couldn't even remember. Benny had not yet been born; in the photographs our mother's jacket sits high on her belly and she crosses her hands like prayer in front of it. Which makes me suddenly sure that I'd last seen them after Maeve was born. Before that, well, it was probably when I arrived, and of course I wouldn't remember that.

So it took a baby each time to bring them to us.

For our father to allow them to come for a visit.

I would have liked to think I knew my grandmother's dry-skin handshake when she came over to the class and bent over to speak to me. I would have liked her to kiss me on the head or face instead of a handshake that showed my class what strangers we were. She drew my veil through her hands and said how nice it was and *what a good length, too.* I noticed the other girls' veils, and there were two very short ones that looked a bit silly, alright. We had bought both the dress and veil at a shop that sold other people's clothes. I was terrified that someone in my class would know this, just from the slight prickly smell of too much washing powder. The shop owner wrapped it in a black plastic bin bag and brought the hanger's hook out the top. We had to leave the shop dangling the dress with us, and I couldn't wait to get to the car. But our grandmother liked it, and how the sleeves came down into elastic cuffs and then opened up again make it seem like white flowers were growing around my wrists.

And when she said this I couldn't understand why she and my father did not get along. For this was exactly the kind of talk he came out with sometimes. Words that turned something ordinary into something magical. The question *How can they not like each other* rang so loudly in my head I was afraid that I'd said it out loud.

I looked across the church yard to where our father stood with some of the other fathers. I could tell that he went among them in order to get away. He never really talked to the other fathers. Not outside the church, not at the athletics day, not when they all sat on the bonnets of their cars at the back of the supermarket waiting for us to return on the bus from our school tour to Craggaunowen. He took my hand and immediately began asking what I thought of the crannóg huts and the quern stone they used to crush corn. There were no goodbyes to the other fathers, the kind that fathers give each other: a nod, *Good luck*, a tip of the finger like when drivers signal each other. We got into the car and sped out onto the road and he changed gears as sharply as he talked. Wanting to know if I enjoyed being on *the island settlement, such a sophisticated set-up for those times, unbelievable really*.

What could he possibly have to say to the other fathers outside the church? Maybe he blended in by giving out about how so many people were giving so much money to kids on a day that was supposed to be about *something more important, something pure*. I'd heard this speech the night before. I had an idea that fathers liked to spend time complaining about things instead of putting up with them or trying to do something about them. One of the girls in my class, Noreen, told us all, including the teacher, how her father had *shouted the place down* about how much her mother's outfit for the Communion day cost. And she said the price. I slid my hands down onto my knees, scraping their wetness dry on my jeans. I couldn't look up, for I was sure that everyone would notice my red face. Red because the price was the same as our rent for a month. The woman's dress and maybe a matching jacket would fill the envelope on the kitchen counter. And I started to pray that our mother would find something to wear that might look like it had cost a certain amount of money.

In the photographs her jacket and skirt look a much lighter blue than they really were. Like our faces, it was made pale by the camera and the bleak sunshine after rain of that morning. But it looked as good as the suits of the other mothers. I even looked as closely as I could at the expensive suit of Noreen's mother, to see if I could count all that money in its yellow and orange and gold threads. But all those woven squares made it look like a rug; even the ends of the sleeves were frayed. While I figured out that these loose threads were part of the style, I felt satisfied that maybe not everyone did. Ha. So much for her swanky suit. And I know that I examined my mother's blue suit more than my own dress for fear that some previously unseen stain might have shown up on the big day. Like when you use onion juice to write an invisible letter. I looked to make sure that no small pimples showed on the cloth, the kind I'd seen her shave off our father's trousers with a razor blade.

And even though it passed itself off as a new suit, it wasn't as pretty as our grandmother's outfit. She wore a deep-pink dress that was belted like a coat. Fuschia, almost as rich as the flowers that dripped down the wall outside school. It looked nice with her hair, which was curled in a soft yellow cloud around her face. I felt a bit ashamed that I was more proud of how she looked than of my mother.

Maeve chatted to our grandfather as if they were picking up a conversation from last week. I watched them nodding and laughing. Our grandmother arranged small bunches of us for photographs. Our father came over when our mother went and brought him to where we gathered in a corner. The wall had lots of lichen on it, so much crusty green and yellow that it looked wallpapered with the stuff. The hands of our grandparents laid lightly on my shoulders, light enough to be floating and me imagining their weight. After a few photographs I didn't mind any more that their turning up had turned our father's face to stone. They talked with our mother about where we might go for lunch. Maeve asked if we could go to the toyshop as well; she was sure that I would get her something with the money that sat bunched like little cabbages in my white lace bag. They said, *Maybe, we'll have to see what your mother says. Or indeed, what Eva wants to do on her big day.*

In the end, they left immediately after lunch. I suppose that the broken feeling at the table was too messy even for my big day to fix. Our father had steak and chips and he made long and careful work of cutting the meat and eating chip by crinkled chip, and talking mainly to me. I felt ferociously angry at how he could divide the table in two like that; we might as well have been sitting across the restaurant. But the chips made me sad for him. He put as much seriousness into eating them as he would into reading one of his books about the Bronze Age or how to build a boat. Maeve kept our grandparents busy with her stories. Which meant our mother didn't have to talk too much. She sat next to me slowly taking sips of milk from a big glass. Because the glass had a slightly green tinge, it made the milk look faintly minty, even more cool and soothing than milk itself. I felt happy that she was remembering to drink her milk. She was big on that these days, with the baby.

Maeve was humming about dessert. The waiter had waved a plastic page in front of her: mounds of ice-cream with chocolate running down the side like gloopy rivers down a mountain. I didn't want any. Even if I wasn't full of burger and tomato slices and feeling oniony burps building in my throat, I would have given up on dessert just so we could leave this table. There were lots of First Communion families around us. If I had to be another one of them – this was a game I used to play in my head at athletics day and the supermarket and other places containing families – I would be ... the table with thirteen people. The Communion girl sat at the top like a princess. Her mother and father were at her left and right hands. Down the table, sisters and a brother and grandparents. A lot of talk came from this table. Everyone seemed to be trying to talk to all twelve other people. They got very excited when the dessert menu came their way; it looked like everyone ordered something after a long time of the waiter standing there, nodding, crossing things out as people changed their minds. I'd seen families like this on television. Usually American. At some-body's birthday. Long tables, loud talk.

Our table started to come apart. When nobody else wanted dessert, our mother talked Maeve out of it by promising her an ice-cream cone in the town. On a different day I would have backed Maeve up. And I felt bad as we walked in a line past the big family's table and she stared longingly and lovingly at the plates of chocolate cake and the tall glasses of knickerbocker glory.

I remember that I rarely felt so sorry for my sister as on that walk of hers past the desserts. Protective, wanting to take her shoulders and move her out of their sight. And I think that I must have started growing up just there and then. She hugged our grandparents in the car park and they had to gently untangle her arms from around them. All of a sudden I felt fiercely shy saying goodbye to them, far more so than when I saw them that morning in the church yard. But I think that this shyness was really the creeping warmth of feeling like I could easily cry. It sneaked up inside my chest and made my mouth bitter at the back.

After I said goodbye I ran to the car where our father sat with the engine buzzing and the radio playing plinkety piano. I sat in quickly and then arranged my dress carefully under me. It felt like sitting on a crispy cloud. He turned up the piano a little and spoke as if talking to the piano player and not me, as if he was leaning with his elbow on that piano and lamenting his life. *They never could accept me, those two.* I looked out to where my grandmother, seeming so much smaller now that I wasn't near her, had her arms around my mother. The bump lay between them like the round shrub between the gables of our neighbours' houses in Galway. *I was not, nor ever will be, good enough for your mother.* So he was talking to me after all. I shrank back against the seat, under pressure to think of what to say back to him. If something needed to be said. *You don't know the half of it, and you shouldn't have to. There's no need to cast a blight on your relationship with them.* He scrabbled in the compartment at the bottom of the car door and found a box of cigarettes. He only smoked one every month, I'd say. He put it in his mouth but didn't light it. The piano-playing finished. Drums and cymbals started up, as though a march might begin in the car park at any minute.

Blight.

I took this word from that day because I knew it had to do with disease. Our teacher had given us a page to read and comprehend; it was about the Great Famine – *which means huge,* she'd said, sad-looking, *and not that it was a very good famine* – and how blight had come on the potatoes of Ireland and caused people to starve to death or leave on ships. I would have liked to see a picture of blight. I imagined it as purply-grey, growing like fur on the spuds.

But that First Communion day as I watched my grandparents put on their seatbelts and drive away slowly, slower than a bike, I thought that maybe it could be an invisible disease. Colourless like water, like the tears on Maeve's face.

And now they're coming to visit. In a couple of hours their blue car will arrive softly at the outside wall, moving so slowly we won't hear it. So I station myself inside the living-room window. And wait.

Her mother liked the hairbrush and so Maeve liked the day immediately, even if was rainy. Her mother liked it enough to brush her hair with it three different times during the morning. And she tickled the top of Benny's head with it. Benny's hair is coming along now. For a while Maeve thought he would stay bald forever. A boy in Eva's class had hair so fair that it made him look bald on the sunny day of First Communion. But there is Benny's hair, dark and licked to his head. Often there is crusty stuff among it and her mother can lift off whole flakes of it, big as leaves sometimes.

Her grandparents have arrived. Eva saw the car first and sped off to open the front door. Maeve remembers them from Eva's Communion day, of course, but as they walk up the path she thinks that she should remember them from before then, too. Their faces should be fixed more brightly in her head, the way that if someone covered her eyes now, here in the hallway, she would be able to say what her grandmother's hair looked like and how her grandfather had a large round mark on his cheek, velvety, and brown like a penny.

When she hugs them they hold her for a long time. She thinks that because their arms are thin it makes her feel their hugs more closely. Her grandmother's especially. Maeve feels shut inside a cage. Plus her grandmother is wearing a flowery perfume that is rich and sweet around her neck. After the hellos are finished they go to the bedroom where Benny is sleeping. Maeve follows. Even though she sees him every day, sleeping in that strange way with his arm behind his head as if he is always ready to fight off monsters in his dreams, she never gets tired of how cute it looks. She cannot believe that she was that small once. It would be great to be able to remember what that was like. To return to a cosy time when all that mattered was milk and sleep. At least, that is how things seem to matter to Benny. As she watches her grandparents watching the shivering that runs through his sleep, the tiny sigh of air that he whushes out every so often, she thinks that being able to remember that time would be so helpful when you wanted to escape from things. From feelings like the doll disappearing into the sea when Eva threw her, and her father having to stop Maeve running in after it. She would have plunged in and let the waves close over her head if it meant bringing back that doll. Feelings like the loneliness of sitting under the stairs with her mother, having to stay still and silent when she knew her mother was crying. Like the fear of shouting in the kitchen last night, and the anger at Eva dragging her back from the door by the hem of her nightdress. Benny protects himself with his arm above his head. Maybe she could try going asleep that way.

But now all she wants to do is open all the presents that they brought. There is a big paper bag down in the hall. Wrapped boxes fill it to the top. This excitement is almost too much and she thinks she might cry. Eva did that last Christmas because of the big doll Santa brought. The doll had curly red hair, and brown eyes that opened and closed, and arms and legs that were almost as soft and warmly solid as Benny's. Eva opened her mouth to say something, and then she was gulping, and next thing bawling loudly. Their father had to take her by the shoulders and get her to stand straight and look at him. *Look at me, look at me, Eva, Eve-een. What would Santa think if he knew you were making such a show of yourself?* And of course that made her cry even more. Their mother was very cross at how he tried to fix the situation. Maeve hoped that whatever was in the boxes would not be beautiful enough to make them cry.

And she wonders when their father will join the group.

Watching them open presents should be something he would like. He could do that clever talk like this morning when her mother opened the presents on the bed. *Oh. Oh my. Oh my-my my-my my-my MY.* Her present got the most attention. *The finest hairbrush that Mister Denman ever crafted. Maybe even his prototype.* He riffed his hand across the bristles. *Yes, yes indeed: this brush is based on the prototype he made in his mother's back kitchen.* For Eva's lipstick and eyeshadow he pretended to be a fashion photographer getting her mother to push out her lips, kissy-wissy, and wink one eye. *Oh, yah, beautiful, yah, that's just great, baby.* She seemed to have fun acting this out. These different voices streamed out of her father like he had a dial to change them.

Then they had hassled him to give his present. He held up a warning finger and said that *all good things must wait* and that it would come at cake-time. Eva said something strange. *That's when Granny and Grandad will be here.* As if they did not all know that. Maeve gave Eva her new favourite look: she had taken it from a mean girl in Adare who shouted at them from a town bench as they passed. *Where are ye eejits off to?*

And when they turned around she wrinkled up her nose as if they smelled like socks. Even though she did not want to remember that particular girl, fat and freckled and nasty, Maeve was happy with herself for taking the look and warping her face round it when she needed to. She used it for dinner vegetables that she did not want to eat: cabbage and turnips. She used it for when someone on the News said something like *three dead and two injured* and showed a picture of cars crushed and snowed with glass, or *the worst flooding in the country's history* and pictures of little brown children on top of metal roofs. For things she did not understand but knew she did not want to happen. For when Eva tried to act grown-up when she sang pop songs, or when she said something silly. And she definitely deserved the look then: they all knew that the grandparents were coming. But what was stranger altogether was what her father said. *Eva, if one more person feels the necessity to remind me of that* ... He looked around the bed, ending with a stare at Benny, as if Benny might open his mouth and announce the same thing. Except, Maeve considered, he would do it in a chirpy squeaking voice like the chipmunks. Alvin! Simon!! Theodore!!! She almost laughed out loud. But that would not have been a good thing to do, not just then. And nothing more was said about her father's present to her mother.

He is not here to see Benny's new mat with the rattles and

the mirror and the patches that open like books. They open the presents slowly, smoothing the paper as they take it off. Eva gets a collection of books in a box. *The Chronicles of Narnia*. Eva reads in a trembly voice. She is so happy with these books. She might even read them to Maeve. On the second time round, though. She always reads stuff to herself first. Like she is making a new friend for playing games before deciding to let Maeve join in. Maeve gets a gardening set: there is a fork and a short shovel and orange pots. And seeds for lettuces and flowers. This might be the cleverest present ever. She wonders what her father will think of it. Lettuces are the kind of thing he would like to have growing out the back. Flowers would make their windowsills look cheery.

He comes in from the shed without having to be called. It's time for cake. It's as if he has a clock in his stomach like the one Maeve has: once five o'clock flashes from the clock in the cooker, he is standing there in the kitchen. He washes his hands at the sink, taking a long time to slip and squish the soap between his fingers. Then he turns around to the table. Maeve feels sure that he is about to burst out singing. His face gleams and he says, *Welcome, welcome to our new abode*. Her grandparents nod thanks and her grandfather says that *it is nice to be here. To see these little treasures*: her grandmother speaks and looks at Eva, Maeve and Benny.

They have brought the birthday cake and it sits like a round chocolate castle in the middle of the table. Maeve cannot wait for the kettle to begin whistling like it is dying of pain, the tea to be made in the bigger pot, the first long sinking of the knife into the heart of this delicious cake. *But wait, but wait, my wife must think I've forgotten her present*. He smacks his hands together. They went to a circus in Galway some weeks back. Maeve thinks he borrowed this from the ringmaster, just like she took her look from the mean girl. That, and the way he stands with his shoulders so far back. She looks to see what Eva makes of this. But Eva is staring at the cake. Staring so deeply it is hard to know whether she wants to eat it or it to eat her.

Her father slides his hand into the long pocket down on the leg of his trousers. He fetches something and dangles it behind his back. He walks slowly towards them. Maeve hears herself asking him not to say, *Ta-dah!* For now she sees how her grandparents look at him. They are uneasy. As if someone has prodded them with a fork but they cannot shout *Youch!* without looking silly.

But he does not say anything. Instead he draws out something that rattles softly. It is a long string of small white shells. Between each shell is a round red bead, almost like a berry. When Maeve leans in she sees that they are berries, dried and covered with tiny goosebumps. Where did he find these, she wonders. She would love a whole box of them, they are that nice. He has made a necklace from shells and berries and it is beautiful. Could he have any left over, maybe, and then she could get a bracelet.

Her mother takes it and holds it across her hands. She looks hypnotized by the white and red and the thread that you almost cannot see at all. Like the shells and berries are hovering in a circle before her. She tilts back her head and gives him that deep blue look that Maeve does not see too often. It is like there is nobody else around. It is like the sea calling him in. She wants him to put it on over her head.

I'll take these off for now. Maeve watches her hand flutter at her throat. The pearls that her grandmother and grandfather brought for the birthday. They are perfect and identical and Maeve thinks she would like to have small round teeth just like these. Sitting in rows in her mouth, nice and smooth to lick with her tongue. That is when her father notices them. He bends over and looks closely, and then he looks across the table. Maeve's grandmother has made herself as small as can be; Eva almost looks larger. The shells and berries hang in her father's hand. Maeve hears them clip the floor as he leans lower and further over the table.

I thought we made it clear that we didn't need your kind of extravagance. I thought that was understood. Maeve's grandfather looks like he might cry. There is something all wrong about this, she knows, but nobody can do a thing. When she thinks her father's voice might get louder, it does not. It softens and swoops low. When he does this it reminds her of the wire game where you have to move a wand around its curves and dips without letting it buzz. *All we want ye to understand is that we are a self-sufficient family. Things like pearls have no place in our ... our world view.* Eva stares at Maeve: she too is thinking about the presents in the living room, if they belong with the pearls in his way of seeing things. Their mother looks down at the pearls on the table. They could be round white tears from her eyes, she looks that sad. He brings the string of shells and berries over her head; it catches in her hair and he has to loosen it. Now that Maeve knows how important he has made it seem, she does not like it any more, and she does not want a bracelet like it. She wants the pearls to stay.

And they do. They lie on the table like a beautiful snake all through the cake and candles and singing. They are still on the table later that evening when she crosses through the kitchen to the bathroom for tissue to wipe her face before anyone sees it. Her grandmother told her to be a good girl and her grandfather said, *No fighting with your sister* and then they were gone. When she started crying she felt chocolate rising sour and thick in the back of her throat.

But what about if she wants to fight with her father.

What about that.

Nobody said anything about that.

Outside again.

They have not been for a while. But Benny has expected it tonight.

There was something about the way she set him down to sleep that let him know. She left the blanket loosely over him. She did not pat it down each side. She did not spend time speaking over the top of the cot. There was no singing. She did not want him to go to sleep.

She was taking him out.

She lets him lick something thick and sweet from her finger while she speaks to the person he cannot see. He hears that same voice coming from faraway. It gets higher and then squeaky, and she drops it with a clattering noise. And it still talks after them as they move away.

Outside is cold on his face as usual. But he is dressed in more clothes this time. He did not like the feeling of putting on three things on top, his arms getting more and more tightened. He did not like the socks. He did not want the hat. Where could they be going to need all this warmth?

He hears the big whispering sound again. But this time it gets louder. They are moving to it. Will he find out what it is this time? They are getting closer and closer.

His mother's hair starts to flap all around and it wraps itself across his face and it slips between his lips. He has to get it out. It feels like it will fill his mouth and then what will he do because he will not be able to cry to tell anyone.

She knows that he is afraid and she draws her finger over his mouth to loosen the hair. But still it blows in the wind, more and quicker, until Benny feels like he is inside her hair. Hidden in there. Nobody will find him.

She is walking slower now. Whatever is under her feet has changed from a crunching, cracking sound to no sound at all. She walks thickly. She is pushing the ground out of her way. Out of their way.

And then they stop.

And she sits down. The big whispering sound is so close now they must be inside it. It must be listening to them. She sets him in front of her on her knees. Wraps her arms around him and puts her chin on his head. He is wearing a cap and a hood so it does not feel heavy. She speaks for a long time. Her voice is that same voice, always dropping soft words to him. Like food on a spoon. She takes away one arm and uses it to do something. Then there is something cold rolling against his cheek; she presses and moves it with her hand. He tries to catch it. When he touches it, it feels like one of his rattles. The one with the small balls on it. But it also feels cold enough to have come from someplace in this dark dark whispering night. Whatever it is she puts into the most inside pocket. And buttons up all his coats again. He hears rattling from her neck. She folds him inside something else. Something of hers. It has her smell.

She lays him down. She speaks one more thing.

And then she is not near him any more.

He hears the big whisper get huge and loud. Like a roar. Like a hungry belly.

Storm

First the crying sounds like we all know exactly where it's coming from. *There, there,* and we move together into the wind. The morning has a bloody rip across the bottom of the sky. And it's salty in our mouths from all that sand blown at us. But then the sound comes from behind, curving round us like a boomerang, and we turn back over our right shoulders. It's so hard to pinpoint where. We don't have clues about strangely shaped rocks and the number of steps to walk west and then north like the treasure map our father helped us to make last week.

He looks like he might dig up the sand with his bare hands or move all the rocks from where they sit in a long black heap.

And if that doesn't work he might walk into the sea.

His face is set as hard as one of the rocks. His chin juts out as though it's the thing leading us through the wind and biting sand. The tip of a ship or an airplane. We follow him with cold faces and empty stomachs and something sickening growing inside us.

The only other time I've been awake this early was when Benny was born. I remember thinking how strange it was that babies could arrive at any time of night or day. For them time didn't matter like it did to people working in offices or to us in school watching the snaily creep of the clock. There was a time to begin and finish the day, and after that time to be at home and watch television and read and go to bed. But babies could decide to look for a way out of their mothers at two or three or four o'clock in the morning. It seems that that was what Benny decided on. I remember our father waking Maeve and me and saying, *A brother a brother girls ye have a brother.* I reached for my watch and pressed the button to flood green light onto the numbers. It was half past five. I had never seen that time before, not even when different troubled things kept me awake late and kicking the sheets into big dunes at the bottom of the bed.

Half past five. This would be when bakers in Galway city are working on the day's loaves and cakes. I used to think I wanted to be one, getting up in the dark and having most of my day's work done when other people were settling into theirs. It seemed like great freedom, and a nice-smelling job too.

Benny came to us at half past five and now we are out looking for him. We have fanned out again, this time walking the length of the rocks. The sea never comes up this far, as our father showed us one day when he walked the blackish line where the tide raced to and stopped and then later turned round. So the bits of rubbish around the rocks aren't brought in by the sea, but left there by people who don't have any manners. Coke cans and Tayto crisp bags. We would never be allowed to leave things like this behind us. Our father had very strong opinions on *wrecking the planet. Kill a bird, that ring-pull would,* as he picked up the piece of metal and ringed it on his thumb like the thing he used to play the guitar. When he used to play the guitar: a long time ago.

Maeve shouts that she thinks she's close and we cover our length of ground and catch up to her. Our father drops to his knees and looks like he is going to crawl into a crevice. I hear Benny now, louder because he is nearer. But it's not a wild panicky cry. It doesn't even sound that much different from when he's announcing his hungry belly. Then he is in our father's arms. He is wrapped in our mother's green Aran cardigan, the one Robin sent her for her birthday.

It came three days early in a soft bulky package. She opened it in the kitchen and told me who it was from. Maeve was playing with Benny in the living room, and I know that's why she spoke Robin's name so easily. *But we won't tell your father, alright? For now. Only because he'd love a cardigan like this and maybe Robin would feel under pressure to send one to him too. And they're awful expensive.* She pressed it to her face like you see people doing in television ads for washing powder and how nice it has made their clothes. Even though it looked rough and scratchy, all that thick wool and big clumped stitches, it was really quite soft. I took the cuff between my fingers and rubbed it. The buttons looked like horse chestnuts with the sign of the cross cut into them, like our mother marked her bread for the oven.

It was a thick rich forest-coloured cardigan and it looked beautiful on her. Especially with the colour of her eyes. On the day of her birthday I wished I thought a bit more about the right colours of eyeshadow. I hadn't thought about any kind of green, but Robin had, and it made our mother look like someone famous on their holidays.

I didn't know what she would do with a cardigan as nice as this one, a cardigan that she wasn't going to wear because it might cause trouble. I looked at the stitching, the complicated way it crossed over and made designs that looked like berries. Maybe when I got older I could wear Robin's cardigan. And pretend he had bought it for me. And not just sent it in the post but put it on my shoulders. My eyes travelled all those stitches and thought that whatever secrets there were between our mother and Robin might be as full of twists and turns as they were.

Benny peeks out from the forest green. He looks surprised to see us. As if we are not the ones he was banking on finding him. Our father smushes his face down into Benny's and he says *Ohmygod ohmygod* from inside the wool. Over and over again. Thick words, and more frightened than I ever heard from him.

Behind us the tear in the sky has opened to fill the world with soft orange. The morning now looks kinder than it had done when we set out. *With light comes hope.* Words from one of the priest's slow drawn-out sermons. I hear his voice as clearly as if he's standing here on the beach with his arms held out like he too wants nails put into the palms, just so. I realize that it never occurred to me to pray that we would find Benny. Probably because our father didn't suggest it. Not the way our mother would have done. *Say a Hail Mary, girls.* I'd heard this for all sorts of situations: the car engine shuddering and giving up on the way out of the shopping-centre car park, all those times our father announced that he was thinking of applying for some job in the paper. And the first day he set out for his new job of driving the fish lorry. She took our hands at the front door and squeezed them tight, like she was trying to squeeze the most serious and deep prayer in the world from them.

Say a Hail Mary, girls. And sometimes we would say it out loud, in our low solemn church voices. Other times we'd say it to ourselves. Except when Maeve's lips moved she really was praying, while I was just pretending. Like someone in a black-and-white film on television with the sound turned down, I made my mouth move more energetically, rounding and lengthening the words.

For more serious matters we had to say three.

Three to me just blurred into one long and boring begging

chat. I forgot where to end each and begin the next. So I followed Maeve, *Blessed are thoungstamunwomen*, right to when she blessed herself with hard clips of her forehead, chest and shoulders. One time I finished like the magician showing that there was nothing hidden up his sleeves or in his palms. I even pretended that I had little white gloves on and I pinched the tip of each finger to pull them off. Our mother wasn't amused and she told me that if I felt it was beneath me to pray that the hot water would come back in time to bath Benny, well then I needn't bother next time.

Next time what.

Next time there's no money for the school tour to Belfast or stringy tough meat in the stew. I could do my multiplication tables by that stew: five times more carrots than pieces of meat, all bobbing in ten times more gravy. Or our father calling Robin *a smart-arse do-gooder*, which he did the day after the shed was built and our father seemed suddenly to hate the fact that his best friend had helped with it. I did think about praying away these things, or at least trying to soften them a bit. But there wasn't any point, because such things stuck and made us the family that we were. It would be like praying that the colour of my hair would change to blonde during the night, like Maeve's, and then maybe everyone at school would be so dazzled by it they'd forget to make the joke of the day about my limp.

Next time our mother leaves the house in secret and brings Benny with her and leaves him for us to find but no way of finding her.

Because that's what's shouting through my head above the wind above our father's *ohmygods* and the sounds he makes like drowning.

Maeve brings home a big orange shell in her pocket. It has a piece missing from it, which makes it jagged against her hand when he slides her hand in to touch it. It has lumps like little warts on it, and they feel nice to rub with her thumb. They are walking in single file, like the way the kids have to do outside Eva's school. Her father in front, carrying Benny. She is in the middle, and Eva so far behind that Maeve keeps having to turn around to make sure she is still there. She thinks that the sea brings things home, like this shell, but it can also make things disappear.

How are they going to find their mother?

The wind is stronger now and it feels like it will get bigger and bigger during the day. Maybe even take roofs off. Like that time they saw the wavy metal roof of their neighbour's shed in Adare fly over the wall and into the field and land like a magic carpet. She wants to run on and catch up with her father, but then she doesn't want to let Eva slip any further back, so she stays in the middle as equally as she can. Anyway she thinks that her father wants to be with Benny and only with Benny as they walk home. She can see the house now. The living-room light is still on, and it looks strange because the morning is now bright and the light inside is trying to win over it.

She would like to see her mother move into the window.

For a second she feels sure she sees someone in there. A shadow across the light. But nobody looks out at them. The windows of the house seem grey and lonely, like the empty house is begging them to come back.

And there is nobody in the kitchen and in the bedroom and in the bathroom when she runs around to search. Eva shouts at her to *stop it Maeve will you* but she knows that she should check everywhere. Wardrobes and under beds. Behind the long curtains pushed aside in the living room. People can be tucked in all sorts of places. Benny was under the rocks, after all, and her mother used to hide under the stairs. With Eva shouting even louder she runs out to the shed. But her father is already there and he has found nothing. He sits in the middle of the floor and stares at the wall where his tools hang. He has no answer to this. There is nothing in a book that can help them. She thinks about sitting beside him but he has a look on his face that says, *Don't come near.*

When she goes back to the kitchen Eva is on the telephone.

She must be talking to someone she knows, Maeve is sure, for her voice is normal. Not shy and confused like the time she had to ring someone in her class about where to buy the schoolbooks.

Okay. Yah.

Okay.

Yah I will.

We don't know what time.

Our da woke us up because he got up to go to the bathroom and she wasn't there. And then he said that Benny was gone too.

No Benny looks grand.

Eva turns away. Maeve follows her. Eva gives her a cross look. Then her face takes on a sly secret look. Like she has stolen something.

Benny was wrapped up in a big green cardigan. An Aran one.

Her voice changes too; there is a little click in it now.

Yah that's what happened.

Yah that's everything, Robin. That's everything I can think of.

Maeve has never seen Eva look so much like a grown-up. But not a grown-up she knows. A person with a tough face and a voice for dealing with trouble, or making more trouble than there already is. This is a strange Eva to see. And it is Robin on the telephone. Maeve supposes that Eva thinks he might know where their mother went; maybe she went to his house.

Maybe this and maybe that. They cannot answer firmly like the woman on television who won the car when she was telephoned. She said, *Yes, yes I'm sure* and then started shrieking with happiness when she was right.

Upstairs Benny is asleep. Will he dream about his adventure,

Maeve wonders. Would his dream tell them everything they need to know?

She does not like that their father is still hiding in the shed. Doing nothing. There must be other ideas for how to find her mother. He should telephone her mother's mum and dad and see if she is there. Maybe she missed them so much after they left, after they let her give them a chunk of cake, that she just had to go there. But the car is still outside the house. If the car could talk what information would it have? And there is the story of Benny under the rocks. How could that happen?

Rain has started and it pelts down harder and harder. Even the sea would feel jabbed and hurt by that rain. The weather forecast last night said High Storm Winds and she cannot remember how many Inches of Rainfall. She remembers this now as it screams wickedly against the side of the house.

How could that happen?

The fright of it starts to pile on top of Maeve like rocks. She cannot breathe properly and she scrabbles at Eva's arm for help. Eva is off the telephone and trying to make tea. She has Maeve sit down and she shows her how to draw the air in through her nose. Maeve does this, and it works because she imagines that the air is like a soft white scarf that she is rolling up slowly. Eva talks steadily to her; she says that Robin is coming soon and he will help them. *Everything will be okay*, she says. *It will. It will. Don't worry.*

Soon Maeve feels alright. At least as far as breathing is concerned. But there is a high wind outside and her mother might be somewhere that she cannot breathe at all.

What are they going to do?

Hail Mary.

Full of grace.

She starts to choke on it.

Benny wakes.

Is he still there, out there in the cold place?

For a moment he thinks he is, until his eyes get used to the familiar things around him. The red whirl hanging above him. The blanket that still smells of when he spilled all the new different-tasting milk out of his mouth onto it.

The cold place was only cold on his face, that was all. The rest of him felt warm. He knew he was awake there. But it was so dark he could have been asleep. He knew he wanted to stay awake, even though he was tired and sleep was hauling at him. He wanted to stay awake because he did not know this place and what strange sounds and hands might come for him in this dark.

But he was not able to move his arms and legs in that place. She had wrapped him so so tightly in the big blanket that smelled like her. When she tucked him into that place and he heard her leaving, the soft thumps of her steps and the rattle around her neck, he knew she would not come back to take him out.

He turned his eyes as far back as he could see, but all there was was dark. He smelled something like dinner on the air. His belly started to call at him. And that was how he knew he would stay awake.

He waited as long as he could.

And then he started to cry.

It sounded different in this place. It came back to him, all around him. It did not fly up and out like his own crying. It fell down on his face. That was when he felt more afraid than he had ever known. The fear that he would cry his hunger as much as he could but nobody would come to feed him. He would not feel hands scooping him up and saying soft things to him. That was when he wanted to fall asleep.

But they did come and now he is here with the red whirl above him and the blanket he knows. He cries out and it frightens him.

So loud this time it hurts him to make the sound. He keeps going until he hears steps coming to him.

And then he stops and puts himself back to sleep.

He does this many times through the night.

And someone always comes.

We drive past a farmhouse with slates missing and a boat pulled into the space by the gable where a tractor or car might usually be. The hull is licked with green, grades getting darker down toward the bottom, and the mast rises higher than the house, topping it nearly twice. One of those things that might look even stranger if it was down closer to the town: the kind of house containing the kind of person that kids persecuted. But we're still in rougher country. And I feel like there might be all sorts of oddities in this landscape.

I saw a television programme recently about an artist in America who filled the land behind his house with giant sculptures. Except they weren't marble or wood. His structures were built from girders and old farm equipment and massive tracts of sheet metal. One stood twenty feet high with old axles set in like eyes. Or at least that's what I thought. I was probably looking for something that made this ugly rust-clad thing likeable and sympathetic in some way.

That, and the fact that it reminded me of the book our father once read to us. The Iron Man. *We loved his largeness and his loneliness. Wandering around not really able to figure out who he was and what he was for.*

I wouldn't have been surprised to have found something like that built at the back of our father's house in the woods. Something to keep him company in the making of it. But a creature he might easily have turned on when he was finished.

The garda hasn't noticed the boat. Or if he has he hasn't found it as strange. Not pass-remark-able. Linda's turn of phrase for when we saw somebody worth investigation in a nightclub. His eyes sweep the road in front of us. I imagine that they see everything, would notice the first little step of a rabbit from the under-growth, swerve to avoid it.

His steady gaze reminds me of the garda who came out that night in Barna.

He came only after we'd begged our father to call for help. Robin was already there. All of us, Robin, me, Maeve with sad serious nods of her head. Benny with his crying even though he had been fed and changed, crying that would break your heart if you listened closely enough to hear the crack in it. All of us forced the phone call.

A person has to be gone for twenty-four hours, or is it forty-eight, before they'll entertain it as a missing person.

That evening I felt the cords in my arm tighten and wind up to punch him. So hard, I said to myself. I thought to hit him, there and then, in front of everyone. Our father and his knowledge of everything. Details stored in his head like those little drawers they had in the library. The way he could flick through them so calmly while our mother was out there somewhere. Lost.

Lost was the word I had to keep thinking. In spite of the emptiness, it had some hope trailing from it.

Robin looked like his thinner older brother had turned up in his place. He wasn't the Robin we needed. Not the one who could build cabins with one hand tied behind his back and make dates with Saudi Arabian princesses like our father said he had done in America. He looked as frightened — no, more frightened, than any of the rest of us. Maeve included. Who only stopped looking around at us, one by one, in order to restart crying. Robin was more alarming to look at because his face was grey like cement.

I thought then that it was to do with the green cardigan.

He had asked to see what Benny was wrapped in. *Had said it like that, too, as if he'd forgotten what I told him on the telephone.*

Robin was the one who found the pearl necklace in the pocket. I couldn't believe we hadn't come across it. But Maeve and I and our father did not work the cardigan through our hands like he did. We did not press and knead it, let it slide onto the table like slow thick water. Next thing the necklace was in his fingers, and I now feel like all of our hearts must have slowed down to the movements of Robin's hands. Quietly clutching and letting go of the cardigan. Slowly dropping the pearls.

That was what finally made our father go to the telephone.

The garda was nice to us all. He gave especially kind smiles to me and Maeve. He was nice up until he asked our father if we would leave, since there were some sensitive questions to be asked. Robin was implied in that. But our father asked if he could stay.

So we went to our bedroom and stretched our hearing as wide and deep as we could. Below us they sounded how goldfish might sound if you could hear them speaking in a bowl. Words were like bubbles released and drifting up to us, mostly breaking apart before we could make sense of them. Very often voices got high and angry. That was our father, mainly; sometimes Robin. Through it all the garda sounded calm. His voice was the low steady line we could hear running along under everything.

He must have stayed late. For we fell asleep, both of us in my bed. Maeve kicking during the night woke me up. I wanted to get up and go down and see if Robin was still there, if our father was in the kitchen, what kind of help the garda had given. But I couldn't move. Not one fingertip. It was as if what had happened last night froze me to the spot. Like somebody in a fairytale. If I got up I was doomed to see something else bad. And it would happen every night until I told someone.

So I stayed in my bed and tried to swim into sleep. I turned away from Maeve's heavy hot breath. For a moment I wished it was storming outside; I always found it easy to burrow into the bed and let sleep come for me when there was wind and rain outside. The smugness of being safe and sound. But then I took my wish back. Our mother was out there somewhere.

If I spoke now to this garda with the kind face, if I told him things that I hadn't been asked to tell that night, I wonder how he would react. Keep driving most likely. I've seen that in films. Someone in a taxi tells their worst dealings or fears to the person at the wheel. And they help out as best they can by keeping on eating up the miles, getting the car from A to B.

Routine can be so comforting.

Regimen. We use the word in nursing sometimes, but most often light-heartedly if someone is on a liquid diet, or has to drink water for twelve hours so as to float their ovaries and let them bob like fruit in the ultrasound.

Except when our father turned regimen into his life's work after he lost control of things that night.

I have to see what he says about that date in his notebook. I have to see what he knew, or guessed. Or maybe how desperate he felt at knowing absolutely nothing. I find the date alright. It's in there twice: first with the picture of our happiest house in Galway, and then with writing beneath it. The only difference is that the date with the house doesn't mention what day. The second time it's there: 15th of August. *I remember that was a Saturday, her birthday, the day of the chocolate cake and necklaces. But as I read I see that he does not talk about the birthday, or the pearl and shell necklace. Or anything that happened that night or the day after.*

I am thinking about the night that I first met her. We were in a packed bar. I seem to remember that the lights were up higher than usual. As if someone had installed harsher bulbs on purpose. To make everyone see everyone else more clearly. Fridge light. No mistaking things. I remember being glad that that is how she and I met. And not amid the purple darkness and fumbling and wet mirrors of a disco.

It was that hour or so before people start to leave for the discos. There were only two in that town then. The crowds used to stream out all lively and buzzed up and then branch out like forked lightning. I had not been to either of those pits for a long time. I was content to have a few drinks on a Saturday night and maybe head off with the lads for late curry. You could only endure a balti after drinking beer. And we usually went for that. Big men that we thought we were. So big that we made one of us eat balti on the night after he had a tooth taken out. I never saw a grown man scream so much. Big men the rest of us alright to dare him to that.

She was with a group not rushing itself to leave the bar for the heave of the disco. Like us. I suppose we all saw it as opportunity lining things up for us. I let the lads move closer to the girls. They stayed sitting at their table. All of their drinks were colourless. Water or vodka or bacardi or gin. Girls' drinks that chuckled with bubbles and ice. The lads set up camp next to them, waving me to convey our pints over when they were settled. The barman gave me a look that said he thought he was rid of the likes of us for the night. It would have been ideal if he was. The only other drinkers were three older couples who looked like they might have been on holidays in the town. And had realized their mistake in choosing this as their destination and were now drinking steadily and not talking to each other in three corners. He could sell a lot of shorts on their despair.

As I leaned on the bar and looked around me I felt supremely glad that once the idea of America was in my head it made everything else easier to endure. The town was a godforsaken spot. I would miss the lads but only for a day or two. Not as much as they would miss me. My empty stool next to them would remind them of the balls they did not have to take their chances in New York or Boston or San Fran.

I brought the drinks over and one of the girls said that I had great balance to be able to carry three pint glasses between two hands. I lowered the cargo of Guinness onto the table and sat in the empty seat next to the girl that I had noticed did not talk as much as the others. She seemed content to be amused by them. She was not committed to their shrillness and big swinging laughter. But she nodded and giggled softly at all the right moments so as to remind them she was still in the gang.

And that was what I liked about her. Without even knowing her name. The gentle laugh. A laugh that could be mocking them for all they knew. She did not drink as quickly as they did. And then I realized that she did not drink at all, for when she was invited to another she said, 'Same again, 7-UP.' She was the driver for the night. The other two were her cousins. Sisters but you would never have guessed it, they were that different in looks. And she could not have been more different if she had been a film star hanging around with factory girls. I felt bad when that thought announced itself loudly in my mind. But I knew I thought it because I was so taken by the look of her.

And suddenly I did not want the lads to start manoeuvring this group. The mathematics were easy, three for three. But I wanted to figure this out for another time. A better bar. A time when I had not come so haphazardly for a drink. I felt like there was still sawdust from the site in my hair. My hand on the glass looked huge and cracked. I took my courage in with a big gulp of the pint. I started to make a plan with her. With luck the others were so well on that they did not notice.

That is how I met her again six nights later. Belinda. She had a wedding to go to and I was her company. And that was that.

I am writing this sitting in the window of our bedroom in Barna. The breeze from the sea presses against the glass. I can feel it coming in just a tiny bit. These windows are old and weather gets past them. This is her second night gone. Tomorrow they will start a proper search, even though the guard was good enough to see what he could do tonight. I saw in his face that he was confused as to why I did not ring him sooner. Even though they could not act. But I got from him a look that said if I was a good husband I would have telephoned much sooner. I would have started shouting at them on the phone. Called them a useless shower of fuckers and is this what this country has come to with bureaucracy. He had my measure alright, that Garda Fallon.

I am writing this because Robin thought it would ease me a bit after the guard had gone to stay and drink whiskey and ask me things. Like what it was like the first time I met her. I gave him a bogus version. Because I did not like the sad greedy blue of his eyes as he leaned forward to hear about the Belinda he did not know.

Robin must think I am the thickest brick there is.

I know she was wearing a cardigan he gave her.

I know too that she was wearing the necklace I gave her.

Except that she left the cardigan around our son and the pearls from her parents in his pocket.

Because she is gone I know that it is the most important thing in the world to have self-control. I could not pull Robin by the collar across the table to me and shout into his face. What do you know. What do you know. What do you know, you bastard of a friend.

The words are dug thickly into the page. I see him sitting in the deep windowsill. Awake like I was that night. But he was writing things down instead of just panicking. I wish I could wipe out what happened after that. Sometimes I used to try to pray that Robin had known something or done something. Or even that he had disappeared when she did and that they were somewhere in a secret corner of the world together. When she came back to us it seemed like he was the most heartbroken of all.

And even then, when it was way too late, I did not tell anyone what I saw that night.

After

I stand in front of the mirror on our mother's dressing table and stare at myself as hard as the girl in my class who started the nasty talk about my limp. Then deeper, fiercer. I look for the most hateful thing in my face. I search for the part that makes me want to tear the whole thing off like a Hallowe'en mask when it gets too breathy-hot and stinky inside.

And I know what it is. My eyes. I can't even get a grip on them in the mirror. They keep looking away, skidding off to the side. They are the eyes of a liar.

I should poke them out.

Then I would be blind and lame and our father and Maeve and Benny could abandon me in the city to beg on the street. Like the woman with a missing hand who tapped a tin plate with the tip of her raggy slipper. *Give Me Something,* her toes said. She didn't look like she wanted people to feel sorry for her and wonder how she lost her hand. She fixed them with the blackest eyes I'd ever seen and made them feel bad about themselves and how greedy they were bustling past her with big bags of shopping. It was like her eyes told them they were all going to hell.

Give me something.

I could lie on a doorstep in the city and make friends with the skinny stray dogs. We could be a sort of gang, me and the dogs. And I would forget my family like they would forget me. When it rained by night and when teenagers jeered at me and when guards came and shouted to get up and move on somewhere else, I would laugh and laugh like a witch. And I would welcome more of people's meanness, more freezing wet weather, because I deserved it.

And my eyes that saw her unlatch the back gate and walk into the darkness with Benny in her arms four nights ago: they would be gone. I would only see things as I chose to roll them down inside my eyes. Remembered pictures that I would learn to switch off like lights in a house.

My fault.

I was the last safeguard against what our mother did, and I had not shouted or ran after her.

And this morning she returned.

The man with the hole in his throat found her when he was walking his dog on the beach. He came running up to our house. I saw him from upstairs and I knew that he was bringing news. And because it was the man with the hole in his throat it could only be bad news. *Go away,* I wanted to shout at him. *Go to hell. You and your horrible hoarse voice. You're the devil. Go away.* When our father opened the front door I threw myself against it trying to keep the wheezing man out.

Then our father took him into the kitchen and shut the door on me.

The guards came. One car to our house, the other down to the beach. Then an ambulance. I knew that we wouldn't be allowed to see her. When someone went into the water they didn't come out looking like themselves. How could they, with the waves slamming so hard and the rocks lying in wait. I concentrated and made it into a slow-moving picture.

From a far distance someone is looking down along a beach. There's a low rock with two gulls strutting on it. They start fighting each other to be the only bird on that black wet rock. Then something moves. A piece of cloth. Loosened by the grubbing of the gull's beak. The person looking down the beach knows that he should go down and investigate.

Something is not right about the shape of this rock.

It starts to look too soft and shapeless to belong to the seashore's rough edges. Even the big dirty-white birds seem to cop on to that. They now walk around it with short confused steps, heads tilting to one side.

The person running down the beach scatters the gulls. They take off with shrill yelps. They sound like they're saying, *Go to hell, go to hell, ha ha, ha ha.*

Snow White was dead. But she was not dead. She only looked dead.

Maeve hunts for the old battered storybook, the one with the green cardboard cover gone soft and wrinkled at the corners. She has to find out how this went. The story that she remembers her mother reading to her. The story that her mother said was *a bit frightening but only in the parts about the wicked Queen.*

Her grandmother and grandfather are downstairs. It is late and they have been here for a long time. The crying has stopped. Eva is still down there. Maeve is supposed to be asleep. Her grandmother brought her up to bed and sat next to her and rubbed her hair. She said that her mother was *gone on a long journey* and that Maeve wouldn't see her until it's time for her *to go to heaven too* and did Maeve understand that. Maeve tried to nod hard and definitely. Which felt strange because she was lying down. *Yes. She is dead.* Her grandmother stopped the hair-rubbing. *She got dead in the sea didn't she.* Her grandmother's face seemed to melt. Pink ice-cream softening before it ran into a puddle. Maeve put her hand up to touch her grandmother's cheek. It was wet and red across the top. *We won't say dead, Maeve. It's a very hard word.*

Now that they are all down in the kitchen, Maeve stops pretending to sleep. She gets up to root out the storybook. It's not among the books on the shelves between the beds. Or under Eva's bed. It's so old that it must be with the toys they don't play with any more. She tips forward the big cardboard box at the bottom of the wardrobe. Dry tickly fur and bells and wheels and one-legged dolls spill out either side of her. She kneels and puts her head into the box. There are books in here. Mostly bath books, the ones with only three pages, thick and padded. She used to like playing with them.

When she finds the storybook it feels like finding the treasure in a story.

She can follow some of the words because she has been taught to read by her father. Moving her finger under them as slow as a worm. But she has no time for that now. It's the pictures she's after. The pictures next to each other where Snow White is lying dead under the glass and then she is sitting up, the glass cover lifted to one side and the prince smiling hugely at her. Like she is a surprise for his birthday. Like he will lift her out and carry her around for the rest of her life.

She knows from her mother reading the story all those times that Snow White was not really dead. It just seemed like that because the piece of poisoned apple jammed in her throat. But looking at just those two pictures Maeve thought that yes, you could be dead and alive. If it was only down to the quick change between the pictures.

Maeve takes the book into the room where Benny is sleeping. Her mother and father's pillows are smooth and solid, like no head has ever marked them. She sits down next to Benny's cot. In the crack of light coming from the hall she sees his eyes open and fix on her. They are dark and shiny. What the night-time sea would look like if pieces of it were in someone's eyes.

She does not want him to cry and bring someone upstairs.

She holds a cot bar with one hand and turns the pages with the other.

She starts to read the story to Benny. And it really seems like he is listening. She hears him breathe steadily like a cat. All the way to the happy wedding at the end.

Words and words and words and words.

They buzz around Benny in the dark.

They make him feel easy again.

If only they keep going.

His sister's voice is low and soothing. She looks at him a lot of the time. She slides her hand into the cot and rubs it along his arm.

Words to make him safe.

Words to make him sleep.

Leaving

September starts with rusty weather. It's hotter than the last days of August, and as dry as the few big leaves that have fallen clutched like hands from the sycamore beside the house. There hasn't been wind or rain since that night of the storm. And it's the time of going back to school, but we haven't. Maeve should be starting, but our father has said nothing about it. No new books, no dragging out my big schoolbag from where it lies mounded with shoes at the bottom of the wardrobe. We let the first week of school slide past us like a slow-moving bus with people inside staring out at us.

I wonder how many in my class already know what happened. And how much they would make it bigger and worse. Although I don't know how they would do that, because it was something so awful that I'm sure their parents didn't allow them to talk about it at home or ask questions. The fact that I'm not back in school probably means that they'll be silent when I do return. All talked out. It will become another story, this time hanging over my head like the cloud that walked with a boy in the next class down: his father had beaten his mother so hard that she was in hospital for a month.

Even though I hated the feeling, I let myself spend time on gladness that at least my mother never felt my father's hand. Not like that boy's mother did. What I couldn't understand was that she went back to live in that house. She collected him from school every day. She seemed nervous of all the kids pouring out through the gate. She stood there with her arms wrapped round herself. If you saw her from the back she would look like she was wrapped in a loving hug.

My mother would turn into whispered schoolyard words eventually, I supposed. And she would be all the more frightening because she wasn't outside the school any more. She had gone and the other mother had decided to come back. Why had that mother come back? She looked so sad and anxious. Grown-ups make all sorts of decisions that we can't figure out. We just watch and listen and hope that someone will scatter little bits of information for us to follow. Like Hansel and Gretel all the way to the witch's house and the blazing oven.

When grown-ups make decisions sometimes they announce them seriously, like a judge.

Robin said that he wouldn't be visiting any more.

He said this on the day after the funeral when he came to the house to take the green cardigan that our father said he had to take, *Take it away from me, for the love of Christ.* I found them in the front hall. Robin was pale and hungry-looking. I hoped we could invite him in for some of the sandwiches that were left over from the mountain brought by a neighbour we didn't even know. She was a big lady with red hands and a teary voice. She called me and Maeve *little loves* and stayed until we'd eaten two triangles each. Our father moved around the kitchen pretending to be busy, but there was nothing to do.

But Robin didn't get any of the sandwiches and he left quickly. He placed the cardigan over his arm like it was a towel and he was about to cut someone's hair or serve them food. He called Maeve and me over with his crooked finger. *Garls, it'll probably be a while before I see ye again. So I trust ye'll be good and look after yer small brother.* And then I was crying and very quickly it was louder than at the funeral and I couldn't get a hold of it. Robin held my face in his hands and shook it softly from side to side until I felt like laughing. I wanted to tell him that I wished we could go with him.

He'd told us to look after our brother. He didn't say anything about our father.

And that was that. Robin's old van scatted up gravel and left in a poof of dust and smoke.

That day our father told us that we would be leaving too. *We can't stick around this place any more. It's not good for any of us.* We would move to another town and he would get a different job and we would make things new again. But even with all those pieces put in front of us, it still didn't sound like something that would happen the next day, or the next week. And so he tried to talk about it for longer than we needed to hear. His words turned into flies moving through the air in circles. Weightless. They didn't make me believe in them. I thought to stop him and tell him that we'd prefer to stay where we were. The house. Even the school. But most of all the beach. Because that was the only place that Maeve and me could visit.

Our mother was buried in the graveyard where her long-dead relatives were. There wasn't even a fight about it. Our father gave in because he had nowhere else better. His own mother and father were buried in Ennistymon. But something made him feel a thousand miles away from that place and those graves. I heard him tell this to our grandfather in the kitchen during a night of awful plans to do with our mother. It was the first time I'd heard them talk without bitterness, or our father raising his voice to a nasty height. Her coffin would be closed. No flowers. Quiet funeral. No newspaper notice. Even then it made sense to me that she be buried with her own family.

But it made me slip out from behind the table where I sat with nobody noticing me, nip across the kitchen and hold our father's hand. I wasn't used to seeing him without an argument or an outraged voice. He seemed even more confused than we were. And he was the one who always knew more. We would have to look after him now.

He didn't cry at the funeral.

But he did that night. Very late and in the house's blue darkness. It was one of the most frightening sounds I'd ever heard. One time he read a story to me about the selkie woman who was really a seal and wanted to escape from her family and return back to the sea. He made low sore noises to accompany what the page said about her crying from loneliness and trying to call the seals to be near her. As he read further his sounds grew wider and lower. As if the selkie was trying to heave everything up from the bottom of the sea. And those were the sounds he made that night. When Maeve stirred beside me I put my hands over her ears.

Maeve says she will pack the plates and cups. She has watched her father wrap one in a page from the newspaper. She likes how the print folds and crumples to make new shapes when it is turned around the plate or choked into the cup. Like crazy news. She begs him to let her do it. Even though he says he is sure that she will break something. These are the heavy dinner plates that they do not use. They are older than Maeve.

But he gives in, because he has other things to prepare. He begins taking down the small square paintings that her mother hung in a line of five on the kitchen wall behind the table. That was easy, she thinks. Those pictures are easy to fit in a box. Now the plates: they have to be set down gently one on the other. The paper crackles gently as it squashes under the weight of the next one.

He brings out two lamps from the living room. Their flexes are wound round the bottom. They remind her of the tree near the town, the one with its roots all woven and criss-crossing at the bottom. The tree that looks like it has been trying to pull itself out of the ground. He unscrews the bulbs and motions to her for a piece of paper. She does not believe that the bulbs will survive the journey. One of Maeve's favourite sounds is the one that tells you of the death of a light bulb. Her father shook one at her ear one time: she caught the tiny chinking inside.

They work together without talking. Benny is sleeping after a long morning of crying and pushing away the bottle's teat. Eva did not want to help at all. Apart from her own things in the bedroom, she said that she would not pack a single box. She asked to walk down to the beach. Maeve held her breath at the request. Her father began with a raised voice, *No you most certainly can NOT go* ... But then it trickled away and he motioned *Yes go on* with his hand. Maeve was relieved that he changed his mind, for if Eva was stopped then she would probably still go and then she might not come back at all.

When she came back she had two full pockets of shells and a tiny toy car. Her face was pink from the sun and breeze. She started to suck on a strand of her hair and Maeve thought yuck! because it would surely taste salty. The plates and cups were all packed. Maeve had moved onto knives and forks and spoons. Eva said she would start on Benny's clothes and toys. Maeve wished she had thought of that instead of wanting to do the plates: she loved picking up and smoothing and folding Benny's small outfits. They were bigger than doll's clothes, but not by much. She especially adored his socks, and could not believe that a sock could be so little. It was even funnier that some of them had little cartoon faces on them. Benny's feet were great fun to hold and play with. Sometimes they moved like he was not in charge of them. Kicking out hard in the way her father called his *mule kick*, or flapping like a swimmer's.

As long as she has Benny's feet to play with, Maeve thinks she will be alright. The new house might be nice. But it won't be near the sea. It will be in a town. Her father says that there is a playground near it. *Swings, Maeveen. We'll sit you in them and send you up to the moon.* This sounded silly and she did not like it as a way of making her like the house before she had even seen it. Eva speaks from behind the pile of baby clothes. *I remember a swing. It was a long time ago. I remember a swing in the middle of a park. Was that our first house?* Her father stops rooting out bottles and tins for a second and then crouches even further into the cupboard below the sink. When he speaks his voice is like something from the back of a cave. He says that yes, she's right, there was a swing at the first house. *It's amazing that you remember it, because you were only a nipper when we used to hold you on it.* Eva says she remembers lots of things. She says it in a cheeky voice, like she is being bold to a teacher. *I remember the loud dog. And then all the dolls that Ailbhe had. And I played with her dolls all the time because I didn't have hardly any of my own. And Robin used to bring you home from work. And when he stayed to eat dinner we often had something nicer. I remember . . . I remember . . .* Eva clutched at the little clothes like she meant to start tossing them aside to find something that was lost in the middle of them. Maeve puts down the knives and forks. Her father has come out of the cupboard now and he is trying to lift Eva into a kind of hug. But she is too big and it looks stupid, Maeve thinks, and so it must feel stupid too.

He says he will finish Benny's clothes if there is something else she would prefer to do. *Yeah,* she says, *I'm going in to talk to my brother.* Maeve found this very strange. Neither of them ever spoke of Benny like he was a boy or a brother. He was their little baby and often their toy. Things are changing all the time, and suddenly Maeve does not know what to do with all the forks she has gripped in one hand, all the knives in the other. She must find a place for them. She must open the top of a box and fit them in there. But she cannot let go of either fist, because then things will fall all the way down to the floor. If that silver hits the kitchen tiles, she knows that the sound will make her sick.

Being lifted and passed from arms to arms. When all Benny wants to do is sleep.

His toys and blanket are gathered up. The bear with the bell in his belly makes faraway noises from the bundle of things.

He bumps down the stairs against his father's shoulder. It is dry and scratchy against his face. He longs for her smell in his nose and the taste of her finger in his mouth.

Milk from the bottle still tastes the same, they feed it to him at the times they think he wants it, but Benny does not feel like eating. Everything is different without her. Nothing, no thing at all, is worth hoping for. Because whoever gives it to him will not be her.

Their voices are louder in the rooms of the house.

Things bang and clash.

Doors slap harshly.

Rain patters his face when they go outside.

His sister holds him tightly on her lap when the car begins to move.

I catch my face in the garda car's wing mirror. Shadowy hollows, and my chin jutting more than I like to know it does.

My chin is my mother's, but somehow she wore hers elegantly. Her other features balanced it. Large eyes and a narrow straight nose. I have the nose too, but not the all-important eyes. *If I had those then they would eclipse what the beauty pages of magazines call* a multitude of sins. *Of course they're usually referring to bags under the eyes and pimples and how to hide them. I would like enormous eyes for people to drown in after they'd tripped over my cliff of chin.*

Instead I have my father's eyes. I'm sure I even snap them like he used to when he was impatient or disdainful. Three or four sharp blinks. If they made a sound it might be like the crack of wooden clothes pegs.

I turn away from the person in the wing mirror. I let her face rush backwards against the trees.

We're getting close to the main road now and the garda drives with a bit more speed. I want to tell him that the only time I tried to learn to drive I steered the car off the verge and into bulrushes. Their thick woody stems crackled through the open window, as if they were applauding like an audience growing truculent. Their big brown felt tops looked like microphones ready to interview me about this daft incident. My father removed his hands from the dashboard after the car crunched to a stop. Once he established that it wasn't damaged he started laughing like a maniac. Honest to God, it was so slow and steady it was like you meant to drive us in here. *And he was right. Not about my meaning to, but about the fact that I was veering so steadily and so methodically, and with absolutely no sense of the margin.*

I was sixteen and living with my grandparents then. We were allowed to see our father, but more and more it was just he and I going for a walk around the town or getting lunch in the Italian place with the waiter who called me his darling luffy. *My father used to think that he was* as Irish as colcannon, *that the rippling accent was a* put-on. It gives him an excuse to be lecherous. *I thought this was a hilarious word for him to use. We'd been learning about onomatopoeia in English poetry; lecherous sounded like someone secretly sucking on an orange. But we kept going back and we always had the same things: my father spaghetti bolognese, me lasagna. When I watched him fork deeply into the red sauce and bring it on a mound of pasta to his mouth I thought that he must be hungry living by himself. I knew he shopped once a week, like always, but somehow I couldn't see him attack it with as much energy as he had when* he was trying to save our lives with probiotics and cruciferous vegetables and big flaps of liver.

He would ask me about school and honours subjects. Boyfriends and if there were any. There weren't. My limp had retired to a small and slighter hitch by then, and I wasn't the butt of any jokes at secondary school. My grandmother said that I had my mother's outstanding features and I hadn't a clue what she meant. But I just decided not to stand on the horizon, like the girls in my class who lined up near the buses to wait for the boys to get out of their school.

Instead I spent a lot of effort trying get away from my face.

The face of someone who kept secrets. Always wary. Sometimes I could feel it tighten and sweat on me like a mask. Don't bother with me, this face warned people.

I would look at my father's face over the cruets and the empty candle holders in that Italian restaurant. Trying to see what my mother might have seen when she fell for him. It felt strange thinking about this. But I needed to figure it out.

. And now more so, for the diary has let me know what he thought the first time he met her.

On the days we met and walked around town and ate I studied the older man he'd turned into. I tried to imagine what other women in the restaurant thought as their eyes glimmed over his thick eyebrows and this new beard that wasn't exactly new but always caught me out. And they did look at him: I noted that. And felt sort of proud. He might be living in a cabin but he still made an effort to be trim.

In the places where we'd lived with him there were women who showed keenness. I saw them at the supermarket and the playground, outside school and in the underwear section. They turned to watch us. Some were covert; others stared head-on like we were creatures inside a fence at the zoo. They watched our father lifting Benny onto a slide. Inspecting cereal boxes for the amounts of sugar in each bowl's worth. It took me a while to feel the weight of their examinations. But once I did I felt it everywhere. It was an uncomfortable heat across my shoulders. The occasional meeting of eyes. Questions on both sides. Now it is easier to see it as they did. The man alone, the three children, the lonesome little planet we must have seemed. Something they thought they could fix or feed or warm up.

There were women who offered to hold Benny while our father fumbled with money and shopping bags in the Friday evening shopping queue. One woman who often sat with him on a green playground bench. From the swing I used to watch them talk. She spoke with her face turned to him; he spoke straight into the air in front of him, his arms folded tightly around him like he was holding off cold wind. Her face always looked eager to please, like a saint patiently expecting her prayer to be answered. One time he jumped up suddenly and walked towards us. The woman's eyes travelled with him. We left the playground, and she was already gone. Later I thought that maybe she offered to help us in some way.

Anyone could've told her that you could never get that past our father.

In Newmarket-on-Fergus our nice landlady, the one with the sapphire eyes, set him up with her friend. This friend was a widower, too, she said. Automatically losing points with him, I thought, for even I knew this was wrong, stupid even, and felt like laughing. The landlady and her husband arrived in the car one Sunday night; we could see a third person in the back seat. Our father bounded out the front door. Not because he was dying to meet this mystery woman but because he wanted to speed away as quickly as possible from our eyes at the window. He moved so fast that he looked like he'd been hiding in wait in the porch. Waiting to spring, I said to Maeve. And when she laughed I knew there would be no more of this woman. He was ashamed before he'd even met her.

When he returned that night we were asleep in a tangle on the couch. I woke and saw the television beaming the lurid green of tennis courts onto Maeve's face. Because I was groggy, I burst out with a question about how it went. I said something very cheeky like So what was she like? The kind of tone I wouldn't normally get away with. But he shook his head so ruefully that I wanted to hug him. As if to say, let that be an end to this nonsense.

And it was. And maybe he was lonesome sometimes. But we didn't think about that. And he seemed not to either. Once a new project began, whether it was growing strawberries or trying to teach Maeve and me how to make jam, he had to give it all of his time. Those things seemed to make him happy.

Maybe that's what made me not want boyfriends as much as other girls seemed to. I knew more about self-sufficiency than they did. I was a great ally for all the crying that accompanied their break-ups. The quickest to say something nasty about the girl who stepped in and stole him, the dabbest hand with a pile of tissues from the bathroom and a silvermint. At first their heartbreaks enthralled me: to be that devoted, that drowned in romance. There was a sacrifice in it, I thought. Which eventually turned to delusion, in my take on things. I got bored with them.

There were more interesting lads in my first year in college. Mainly because they were from other counties and cities, and took part in things like debating and badminton: pursuits I couldn't imagine the boys of my grandparents' town engaging in. Away from that town and those boys, I plunged into the scene like it was sport. Enjoyed it but only because I had no problem with extricating myself when things got serious. I didn't like to see that suffering look come over someone's face. Tremulous eyes, like contact lenses slipping loose. I'd end the line before they had a chance to say, There's something I'd like to tell you *or asked me to their home for Christmas. In fairness, I had only one brush with this. He skipped a month of college and came back with a new haircut. In my second year I had three one-night stands and always left first thing in the morning. And I met the nice solid garda and dallied with him awhile.*

But being on your own is better when it comes to managing big demanding things like today's drive up the mountain. You can't have someone fretting for you and trying to help. Help?, *I would probably shout.* How the fuck could you help?

The garda turns to me suddenly and I realize that I've said these words into the thick close air of our car. I shake my head and mutter, Sorry, sorry, talking to myself. *When he speaks I've forgotten that his voice is so mild.* You're fine, you're grand. Talk all you want. *I ask him if I can turn on the radio to the classical station. When it sends a waterfall of harp strings around us he looks pleased.*

I open the diary, which I've been gripping so hard it's left red tracks on the inside of my fingers. Like the marks from the ridged handlebars of that big heavy bike he brought out to teach Maeve and me to cycle.

This is not the home or the town I had intended for my family. But there is a job here in Ennis and there are schools. I lied to get the job and I will make sure that I get Eva and Maeve into the right school even if that involves more lying. I can bring Benny with me to the job for the time being. The husband and wife who own the garden centre tilted their heads to one side and gave me an identical sympathetic look. They are the hippyish type and this helped me when I said I needed to take my son to work with me for a while. Hippyish but well-off at the same time. The place does great business. Especially on Saturdays. That was when I saw the sign on the stone pier outside: Help Wanted. It was unusual and reminded me of America where I used to see it in the windows of bars and restaurants and grocery shops. It made me smile. As if there was no wage involved. Just come in and help us, would you. A sign that you could stick in the window of a house where money was short or a car where an argument was going on. The garden centre sign was an ignorant-looking piece of plywood painted with red letters. You could not miss it.

I wasn't prepared for their niceness. They moved here from England ten years ago and started a very small outfit, growing a couple of varieties of shrubs and flowers for borders. Marigolds and the like. Now it was much bigger and they traded not just with people and their lawns at home but with golf clubs and hotels. They had two other people working for them. Their soft intelligent voices made it seem like they weren't even interviewing me. Just a friendly chat. Which is why I felt bad about the lie once I turned the car out onto the main road with the job in the bag. It was, I suppose, a kind of habit picked up from the months with Robin in America. We got jobs by letting on we could do them, and ten more like them. When the Wrens asked me if I had a good working knowledge of horticulture, I said I did. It was kind of their own fault, really. The question was almost its own answer. Instead of pointing at the drift of white flowers along the top of the low wall and saying, *What's that then?*, they kind of left things up to me. I would study for the job and they would not even know that as a child I stabbed my fingers and thumbs plucking the purple flowers from the heads of thistles, thinking that they were real blooms, bringing them home to my mother. She laughed her head off first of all, and then she put them into a pint glass of water.

As I drove to meet the man who would be renting the flat near the hospital to us, I felt suddenly happy. There were things to learn and a job to go to. Busy again. I sped up because I should not have left Eva and Maeve minding Benny in the playground for so long. That playground was almost all tarmac, too, and I had visions of coming upon them crying and panicking, Maeve with her head split open and Eva holding Benny to herself and trying to draw them all into a safe corner. I imagined other women wondering what kind of parent had left their children alone there. Jesus, I was thinking as I spun through a roundabout, what was I thinking, leaving them there. Anything could happen. The sorts of things that happen these days. Reported in the newspaper. Awful, awful. When I ran into the playground and spotted them straightaway I thanked God as though he had answered a prayer I hadn't even sent in his direction. They were sitting on the bench where I had left them. Watching some boys climbing up on a frame and going hand over hand on the monkey bars. My daughters looked so serious that it made them seem older. Even Benny was grave when I plucked him from Eva's arms.

I have so much work to do to make sure they are always safe.

I am very afraid of finding out how heartbroken they are.

Benny not crying is sadness in itself. And so I am glad that he will be with me and not with some babysitter and other crying laughing babies belonging to strangers.

At various times during my ward training I remembered all the time he spent checking Benny after he was collected from the babysitter's. When he couldn't bring him to the garden centre any more — when it turned out that he thought the woman who worked there wanted to steal Benny, that she had the face of a woman longing so desperately for a baby — he made a painstaking search for a babysitter. But even then he worried. He'd take off Benny's clothes and turn him this way and that to check for rashes. Or bites: insect, animal, human. I remembered it too when a boy I liked in college asked me to roll up his sleeves. Cigarette burns, old dark stamps and newer rhubarb-and-custard-coloured ones that looked like they'd just stopped weeping. His face was still and triumphant, as if all he wanted was someone to see the work he'd done on himself. My father was afraid of something dreadful being played out on poor Benny's wriggling little body.

And when no evidence showed on his skin, my father turned to worrying about what he might be eating. When he found the tiny orange coins of lentils in Benny's top dungaree pocket he panicked. Maeve and I watched him pick through the contents of our baby brother's nappy. He used an ice-lolly stick, and a paper clip opened out straight.

I see him now.

Bent over the table and working in small measured motions, like an archaeologist. He didn't look at all phooey and disgusted by the smell that seemed to ripen as he went on. Benny was nearby in his bouncy chair, la-la-la-ing and grabbing at invisible things in the air. Behind him, against the kitchen wall, were boxes that were still not unpacked even though we'd been in the flat for close to six months.

Our father continued until the search turned up nothing. He dropped his implements into the brown mash and folded up the nappy and bagged it and washed his hands.

Ennis, 1997

Carpets and Country and Western

This time last year I was mad to take the Christmas decorations down. We've been in this flat for a good long time now and I would love to have the whole window covered with tinsel. Big loops of it braiding back and forth. So thick and green that we wouldn't be able to see out. Outside is a small lousy-looking lawn that our father won't cut because he says it's the landlord's job. And the landlord must think that it's our father's job, because nothing has been done and it's growing high enough to topple flat some day soon. I hate the look of it and that it makes us look like the people who abandon old cars and tractors to die at the sides of their houses. The kind of house gables our mother used to call *national treasures*. She didn't make jokes all the time, but when she did it was always something both grown-up and funny to us.

I can't stand this place. When we got to Ennis it was the fastest and cheapest place he could get. So he took it. And these days he's talking about leaving his job at the garden centre because he doesn't like bringing Benny there any more. *Spores and such things. Not good for a small lad.* But there's more to it; I heard him on the phone to the man and woman who run the place. *It's just not on … It's not a comfortable work environment.* The newer voice. The one that makes Maeve and me think that someone else is in the kitchen calling us in for fish fingers and beans. *Girls. Kitchen please and wash the hands beforehand.* The in-charge voice nails words sharply into the air, rap-a-tap-tap. I know that he'll leave the job. Either that or he will fight with someone there and he will be told to go. Thinking about this feels like trying to shoo a heavy dark-grey raincloud away when you want to go out and play.

The place is a bit cleaner than it was when we arrived. Worst of all were the carpets. Well, one carpet, because the sitting room and the two bedrooms had the same stuff down. Big mustard-yellow flowers with brown centres. In our bedroom, Maeve's and mine, we found one place where it looked like grey ashes had been dropped and rubbed in. That explained the smell. Someone had smoked in this bedroom, and I pictured an old man sitting in his pyjamas turning one cigarette after another into long quavering spindles. The kind of thing the television ads warn you about. They always put old people into those ads, too, which used to make me sad, for it looked like smoking and falling asleep in an armchair was the only way for them to pass the lonely night. But now it just makes me mad, because the smell is still here, even though we've spent weeks and weeks spraying lilac Haze and even some sweet expensive body spray from the chemist. It lurks near the wardrobe and then comes at us at night. I wonder if the old man I imagined had to go and have his throat carved out of him like the man in Barna.

Our father and Benny's room has the carpet but not the smell. The first time I saw Benny's cot placed right beside the bed I thought I'd start crying. It didn't need to be crushed against the bed like that; the room had more space than ours. Then one morning I saw it was moved back a bit. And that Benny wasn't in it. He was lying wide-awake next to our father in bed. His eyes fixed on me and I thought he was about to start yelling for his food. But instead he rolled them away from me and fixed his gaze on the ceiling. It was eerie enough to make me feel like I was watching a much older brother. Our father snored on, those small chainsaw revs that we're so used to by now they don't annoy us the way they did our mother. I saw her elbow him a few times; he'd hump onto his other side; tune up a bit and start all over again. Suddenly I imagined Benny jabbing our father with his tiny hand. The thought of it is so cute that I rush over and scoop him out of the aftershave-smelling bed and hold him like I could as easily eat him.

The aftershave is a new thing, like the country-and-western music. He smacks his face with Blue Stratos every evening now, and not just when he's going out for a drink. I can see why he likes it: I tried a bit on my jaws. It feels like ice and smells like whiskey. I even took the bottle and sprinkled a bit on our carpet. It worked for one night.

You know that was the last thing on my mind. He joins in with the man and woman singing that they didn't mean to hurt one another. I find myself liking the song, mainly because their voices are so different. She sings in a sharp doll's voice, with a tiny bit of bossiness in her tone, and he's large and sensible and makes it sound like everything will work out. I think I'd like to see a picture of them. When our father butts in it sounds strange. He has a good strong voice, but singing along with a duet just doesn't work. There's that and *Come On Pretty Baby* and *Rhinestone Cowboy* and *Queen of the Silver Dollar*. He bought a pile of tapes in the second-hand shop and now we're surrounded by songs that make sad things sound sort of alright.

I especially like when he joins the woman singing *I Fall to Pieces*.

The first time he did this he was standing with his back to us and his arms in the sink suds. He started to sing and also move a little from side to side. It looked like he was dancing with her. Singing, to me, is one more way of humiliating myself. There's a lot of it at the new school. None of the good intentions in my head come out of my mouth. I'd love to be able to sing 'Whispering Hope' in class with a girl's version of our father's voice. That'd shut everyone up and make them stare. At this school I don't draw anyone's attention, good, bad, or indifferent. It's so big and I'm a nobody and that's fine when it comes to the limp, but for some reason I'd like to wow them with beautiful singing.

So I started the campaign to have Patsy Cline every evening. I even bought a tape of all her songs for him, but really for me. It's great practice for when I'm older and having my heart broken. *How can I be just your friend* is my favourite line. Our father seemed delighted to have a chance to sing it all the time. His voice gets a bit louder with each turn. Soon he becomes Patsy's singing partner, and they talk to each other in the words, and I pick up the tape and I can imagine her nodding to him and him to her.

You tell me to find someone else to love. And that's when I realize that this isn't such a good idea. He trips on that line more often than he used to. And one evening when he's swaying Benny in his arms and we're sitting at the table mopping up bean sauce with our brown bread, he can't get past these words. He sings them a second time, but Patsy has already moved on. *Someone who'll love me too, the way you used to do.* And then his face is pressed down hard on Benny's head and he's crying and we have mouths full of grainy brown bread that we don't know whether to chew on or swallow whole and go to help him.

This is when I have to stop hating the flat and the high grass.

The carpet and the smoke smell. I have to pay more attention to important stuff, even if it feels queasy. I turn the tape off and make a bit of work of ejecting it and putting it into the box. To give time for Maeve to see if she can do anything. It's easier for my sister and my baby brother to look after him.

And I've tried and I've tried but I haven't yet.

Maeve thinks that the woman who walks over their heads upstairs, looks a bit like the woman on the cassette box. And when she walks it seems she never goes in any other direction except in one straight line back and forth across the room. Maeve imagines her using a broom handle to turn on the television and open the windows. Like the game where you have to stay frozen where you are, no matter what. When Maeve sees her in the hallway she is always wearing a jacket that looks smooth as a pony's skin and has fronds hanging from the sleeves and the bottom. Her face seems drawn like a cartoon: red, red lips and black edges round her eyes. Olive Oyl.

Maeve misses the feeling of her mother's clothes. Here in this flat they are kept in big boxes but she and Eva are not allowed to go near them. Her father has sealed them with lengths upon lengths of brown tape. She would love to find a way to open one of those boxes and close it up again so perfectly that he would never know. She feels hungry for the soft mossy wools and the white blouse with the crackly blue sequins down the front and the skirt with big pockets like buckets into which Maeve used to drop things like flowers, or pennies she found on the floor.

Clothes, she thinks, can tell the truth or lies. When her mother was sad she wore bright clown colours. The jumper with the big circles always made Maeve smile when she saw it. But any time her mother wore it she herself wasn't smiling. The jumper was big and loose, so loose that the neck came down over her shoulder. Lopsided. Maeve knew what that word meant because her mother had shown her how in photographs one of her own eyes was just a tiny bit not lined up with the other. *It's funny, Maeve, how the camera catches that. It's like I'm the devil or a ghost or something.*

And the jumper had enough big coloured circles that you could play Twister on it.

She wants to find that jumper. She wishes she could persuade Eva to take a scissors or a knife to the taped mouths of the boxes until they found it.

Because it would be good protection against the woman upstairs; she could wear it over her head and down to her ankles. The woman is friendly now. She always seems to be coming down the stairs when they are coming in the front door. It's like there's a bell that lets her know. Her father growls once the woman has gone her way. This takes time because she cuddles Benny to her and looks at Maeve's father just like that painting in the church of the girls' faces staring up at the angel. Big up-eyes, amazement. Begging. And they only manage to get away because their father says, yes, alright, she can take the girls to Pennys to see if there are clothes they might like.

And so Maeve stands at a long skinny mirror and looks at herself in a cowgirl outfit. The woman — *Anne, Anne, will ye call me Anne girls, and don't be shy about it!* — puts her hands on Maeve's shoulders. Her red nails look like they would be nice to snap in half, one by one. Maeve stares into her own face in the mirror. She thinks she can see one of her eyes tilting. Blue slipping aside. She looks harder and harder to be sure. Then she sees Eva behind them. Laughing. She is carrying a blouse and jeans and shoes and socks. This, Maeve knows, is more than their father has given them money for. Eva must be planning that Call Me Anne will pay for the extra stuff. And Maeve knows that they will get into trouble. But she sees how Eva strokes the red jeans. There will be no way to tell her no. She herself wants to say no to the cowgirl clothes. She doesn't want to look like Anne, or like the woman on the cassette cover. If she could find a jumper with circles the size of saucers, or a blouse with blue sequins, then she would want something. But she decides to say yes to the fringed waistcoat and skirt, and then look for more things so that it won't be just Eva who gets into trouble.

In the dressing room, with sweet smelly stuffiness all around, she sees in the mirror how they could by accident turn into a family. Anne's fussy hands smoothing the white fringes, Eva giddy and kicking off her shoes. There is another mother telling her girls to hurry on. Maeve is surprised to see that they leave clothes in a messy pile on the floor. Anne seems to like being here in this dressing room, talking to Maeve and Eva in a chirpy voice, telling them that they *look lovely, lovely altogether*.

So it's just as well that her father gets so angry at the amount of clothes they tip out of the Pennys bags. He gathers most of them without even looking at what they are; he rams them back into the bags. Eva gets to keep the red jeans and the shoes with flower buckles; this is because she starts crying. In the yellow kitchen light her slow tears look like butter melting down her face. Most of the time their father will not take tears. They are just not allowed. But this time they work. Maybe it's also the way she holds the jeans to herself. Like a doll or a teddy bear, Maeve thinks. She sees her chance to stuff the cowgirl outfit into the bag. She keeps pink socks and a packet of stripey knickers.

They listen as their father's steps tump up the stairs.

They hear a knock at the door.

His words are not loud, but they are serious, and there will be no arguing with him.

His father beside him like a warm wall.

Benny turns and wiggles to find the best way to sleep. He is not sure about this new situation. Sometimes he is afraid of being crushed. Especially those times his father turns and lifts his big arm and then rests it on Benny. But it does not feel as heavy as it looks. So that makes things safer.

But then there are times when his father's back moves up and down and Benny hears sad sounds from the other side of the wall. Crying like his father is hungry. What can Benny do? What can he do to make this better? He pats the wall with his hand. Soft and soft and then as hard as he can so that his father will feel him there.

Ah my boy.

Ah my small stalwart.

He turns and then Benny is being lofted and held above the world. Then he is landed on his father's chest. Up-down, up-down. He feels the warm movements of his father's breathing.

When will you tell me about that night on the beach?

Cutbacks and False Appetites

He has left his job. He has lost his job. Left, lost, left, lost. You could pluck it out on a daisy. Whichever is true, the thing is that he has no work. Again. First it was the garden centre and the woman there he thought was angling to steal Benny. This time it's the builder who took him on as a site cleaner. When he told us what he'd be doing – sweeping, collecting stray cuts of timber, preparing everything for the arrival of plumbers and electricians and tilers – I knew it wouldn't work out. He's no good with taking orders. The more he needs to hold a job, the worse he gets when it comes to someone telling him what to do. It's as if the whole thing, the job included, the pay, everything, is an insult.

I can't concentrate on things at school. I stray away from the groups at lunchtime. I eat my sandwiches on a bench near the tree that hangs in over the wall. And I make sure to check on Maeve. But she settled in as easily as if she'd been going to school all her life. I'm glad that I don't need to worry about that. Because I have enough to think about. One day a newspaper blew over the wall and into the yard. It was the section with things for sale and jobs. I read those jobs to see if I could find one for him. Something that sounded like he wouldn't be working with a lot of people. I didn't find one that day, and I couldn't understand what some of the ads were looking for, but the whole page made me feel like I couldn't eat any more sandwich. So many places wanted people to work for them. They wanted people to ring the numbers or write to the addresses. Vacancy. Hiring Now. Looking For. It made me think that our father should put in an ad that said No Work Wanted Here. Or one that said Here is What I Will Not Do. At least that would make things clear from the start. I felt so angry that I balled up the page and threw it and my sandwich into the bin.

I still see Anne in the newsagents. That's awkward. She makes me feel clumsy, as if I'm going to knock the stand of greeting cards. Or steal something. I remember never to wear the red jeans when I go there. For it feels like I did steal those. Ever since our father returned the clothes and told her to leave us alone, it's been strange. I try to leave the flat as quickly as possible, I try to get us going so that we won't bump into her. But sometimes we do. And our father is good when this happens. *Anne*, he nods. The word is said the way men driving on the road beck their finger to each other. She doesn't reach out for Benny any more. She doesn't smooth Maeve's hair. Her lipstick looks faded and her high hair sags a bit. I feel bad for thinking anything mean about her. She probably saw us and thought we were a ready-made family for her. I think it mustn't be easy to live by herself in one of these flats, looking out at that same grotty grass, taking the same bockety brick path every morning, and nobody to come home to or make dinners for.

But I have to shut off this feeling, because there's way more to worry about than Anne.

When I see him outside the school gate it feels like no time has passed since Galway and all those weeks that he collected me every day and we looked at something interesting on the way home. Ducks. A display of old doorknobs in a shop window. Water rolling over the weir, bottles and crisp bags ganging in the corners. Anything to make it seem like he was busy and that taking these tours with me was work. His work. But the work of fun and stories doesn't have money going with it, and now the same thing is happening all over again.

I start to pray at night. My prayers cover several things. That a job will appear from somewhere. That he will swallow down his pride and his dislike of people. That someone good will be found to mind Benny. That I can stop holding my breath whenever our father mentions cutbacks.

Cutbacks seem to be the way that we will manage in this time of no job. It mainly involves food. Suddenly fish fingers and beans have become beans on toast. *No bleddy fish in those things anyway. Concocted fish, I'd say. So better off without them.* We get the beans in a dozen tins bought on Friday night at the shopping centre. Bread is now the bread that comes in the white wrapper, the bread in smaller squarer slices. It's much cheaper and he buys a bigger batch of it and we freeze the loaves. And we get the bagged bananas that have an orange Reduced Price sticker on them. I come to hate this sticker. It's a loud shouty orange, and the price is scrawled on in someone's handwriting. We have to eat the bananas in two days, because after that they're gooey and strong-smelling.

He doesn't cut back on biscuits; he's fond of them himself. But we end up getting the ones wrapped in the same paper as the beans and the white bread. There isn't much choice, and we mainly get chocolate chip cookies and pink wafers. None of our favourites.

If we want chocolate bars, he suggests, then we should do jobs for people. Maeve and I look at each other like this is the craziest idea ever. For we don't know anyone. And cutting lawns and walking dogs and washing cars for old people only works for children in books. And how can we do jobs when he barely lets us down to the newsagent by ourselves?

And that's where I get my idea.

Soon I'm standing at the counter waiting for Anne to finish giving back change to a woman with violet-coloured candy-floss hair. Maeve is with me; she begins to count the rows of rolled sweets. I feel sure that Anne is taking her time and talking a bit more to the woman because she doesn't want to speak to us. The woman says, *Oh listen sure that's the way of the world these days desperate desperate altogether lawlessness and no respect for life.* The headline on the woman's newspaper reads, *Four Killed in Separate Weekend Stabbings.* I think how the words *desperate* and *separate* are like brother and sister. Then Anne says, *Yes, Eva?* Immediately my mouth dries up inside. I can't ungum my lips to ask her. Maeve gives my hand a squeeze. Sometimes she amazes with me with her know-how. And I begin to ask Anne if she has any jobs that we could do.

Anne wants to *be clear about one thing.* She wants to give us jobs, but she *won't be accused of doling out charity.* So we have to ask our father before we can *go any further.* I was expecting this. But she wants to help, so that's the first step.

And when we tell him that we have small jobs at the newsagent he barely looks up from his book to inquire. He gets a lot of books from the library. Sometimes he seems to live in them as though they are better places to be than with us. *As long as it's only an hour here and there.* I knew he had forgotten that Anne ran the place. He'd only been in once; after that it was always our job to run down for milk and the newspaper and whatever other small things were needed. He dips his head back to the pages. Looking over his shoulder I see pictures drawn in pencil. The Human Brain. To me it looks like a cauliflower. I think about kissing the back of his neck, but then maybe he'd suspect something and call me in front of him for more questions about the newsagent's job.

And so we go in on Fridays after school and again for half days on Saturday. Anne has us unpacking the boxes of butter and making sure that none of the eggs delivered are broken. I like doing the biscuits. *If anyone asks ye, girls, ye're only helping me out and there's no money involved. Is that understood? Helping Me Out.* Maeve is particularly good at this. When her teacher comes in and sees Maeve putting McVities and Toffypops on the low biscuit shelf, Maeve says, *We are helping Anne out.* Then she looks over at Anne. *We are keeping her company.* I feel myself flush at the lie. But also at the truth of it. Anne waves down to the teacher. I notice that she's wearing her hair down these days, and it suits her better.

And I like the job she has given me: cutting off the tops of the newspapers. *It's called the masthead, Eva, and we return them to show that we didn't sell the newspaper.* I'm allowed to use a scissors that doesn't look like plastic bunny ears; Anne's is large and heavy, and it reminds me of learning to manage the big old black bicycle. Anne says I cut the *straightest freehand lines* she's ever seen, and that's important because you have to make sure all the details are in what you cut off. *The Clare Champion* is my favourite masthead because the letters are big and ancient-looking. I also cut *The Irish Times*, the *Irish Independent*, *The Star* and *The News of the World.* Anne tells me not to be looking through this paper – *British rubbish,* she calls it – and I know it's because of the women without clothes on. But they don't surprise me any more. In fact I feel sort of sorry for them. They're usually kneeling forward and they look hypnotized. Their boobs are so huge it's like they're begging someone to come along and eat them up. And when I see men open to that page before even buying the paper I know that there's something desperate going on, and I wish I was doing Maeve's biscuit job instead.

But my job is what gives the advertisement to me. After I

finish with the *Champions* I flick through the pages. There are always nice photographs of children with their parents out at funfairs or parades. Sometimes they have painted faces. I continue on to the Classifieds. The print is tiny. But I find Vacancies. Groundsman for Dromoland Castle and Woods. There is a phone number and an address. I am about to look for a biro to write it down when I realize that I can cut it out. Because it's in the middle of the page, I must jag the point of the scissors in and cut all round the small ad. I work even more cautiously than I do when making sure to get the date into the clipped masthead.

In the end I decide to cut two. One to leave for our father on the kitchen table. The other to put inside my pillowcase for when I pray that night that he will telephone the number. That he will sound pleasant and interested when he speaks to Dromoland Castle. That he will dress correctly when he meets them: cords and wellingtons and the kind of coat and tie you see on the better-off people on *Emmerdale Farm*. That he will take the job and love it and never want to give it up.

I pray with my hands clutched as tight as on the handlebars of the big bicycle.

And I realize that I haven't said a prayer for our mother in I don't know how long.

Maybe I'm afraid she'll talk back to me.

You must have a false appetite or something, Maeveen.

Her father spoons out more cabbage from the stewy stinking saucepan. Even though she has come to hate cabbage, Maeve knows that if she doesn't eat more of it then she'll be hungry later in the evening. There are no snacks allowed. Milk and biscuits before bed, but nothing between dinner and that. Sometimes he gets the dark green warty cabbage, other times it's the snot-colored one. Neither is any help when it comes time to sit at the table. Cabbage tastes of what it would be like to lick a frog's belly. She doubts that anyone else at school eats as much of it as she does.

She worries that the smell is now on her and that people in her class can get it. Danny Connors always smells of sweet soap. When she kisses his face it tastes of marshmallow. How can this be? His face is pink alright, but still: its sweetness is always a surprise. She kisses her own hand in the play shelter to make sure it's not cabbage. She tries to cuddle up to Danny Connors, who sits like a doll with his legs straight out instead of hanging over the edge of the bench. He lets her squash him into the corner but he doesn't kiss her back.

Walking back with Eva from school all she can think about is how to get more and nicer food. It seems a long time since they had fish fingers or that crispy chicken that she used to love the best. Chicken and chips: her favourite dinner. Mainly for all the crunchiness. But there's no more of that. In fact, there's nothing from frozen red boxes any more and no big awkward bags of chips to push onto the freezer's narrow shelf. Making the bag of chips fit felt like stuffing a doll into a box that was too small for it.

When she'd decided that Sindy had died she tried to fit her into an empty chocolate box. She'd kept it because it had a proper lid that came off with a suck of air, and a purple rosette. But Sindy didn't fit. Not until Maeve bent her legs far forward at the knee and folded them up toward her face. She pushed the lid down. And then she felt the air leave her chest: is this where they put her mother, did they have to break her legs, where was she, where was she, where was she? Maeve fought the lid off and pulled Sindy free and gently bent her legs back to rights.

Anne had given her the small box of chocolates. It was about to go out of date, so it could not be sold. But, as Anne said, *That Best Before Date is a moot point. There's nothing wrong with these truffles, not one whit. Have them, girls, and welcome.* Now that they are helping Anne in the newsagent she and Eva have some money for regular crisps and chocolate, but they have to hide this stuff from him. Sometimes she lets two or three bags of crisps gather in the bottom of her wardrobe and pretends that it's a surprise to find them there. Like presents left in the night. She eats them all together. She likes to mix cheese 'n' onion with salt 'n' vinegar. She eats them in the wardrobe with the door almost closed. In between mouthfuls she talks to her mother. About the biscuit shelf she fills, about Danny Connors's tasty face, about always finishing her copybook writing before everyone else in the class. Making herself slow down so that nobody will give her a jealous look. So that the hour before lunchtime won't seem so long and empty.

About how if her father hadn't been so mean to Anne maybe she and Eva, even Benny, if she made the right food, could eat their dinner at Anne's flat. She has never been up there but she thinks that the presses and fridge would have good things in them. Maeve thinks about food more than she thinks about school. That might be what has given her the false appetite. If you think about things all the time then you want them more. She knows how to make this easier: by not thinking about those things. It worked for a while with her mother. She couldn't bear how much she wanted her. It felt like hunger, but not in her stomach. Up higher. In her heart and further up in her throat. So any time her mother's face and hair and smile slid behind her eyes she shooed them out by blinking hard and fast.

But that's not so hard any more. And she can let her in and not want to taste her.

And anyway, there's another house coming up. Most likely. Their father floods happiness into the kitchen on the evening he tells them that he has a new job. *The kind of thing I've always been wanting to do, girls. Outdoors. Working with nature. Not a soul to bother me.* Eva looks as pleased as if she is the one about to leave school and start this magical job. He has been to the supermarket and there is a block of Viennetta ice-cream. Maeve's mouth fills as she guesses its milky chocolatey taste. It's been so long since Viennetta.

Maybe the time of cutbacks is over forever.

To Benny, everything is beginning to taste the same. His father feeds him from bowls of warm, sea-smelling mush. For if Benny gets the spoon to himself, everything in these bowls will get thrown as far from his mouth as possible.

This is good for you, Benny. I read it in a library book. I found all the stuff and made it myself. Wheatgrass is sort of a miracle ingredient.

Benny keeps his mouth closed.

This bowl has all the constituents a boy your age needs.

He tickles under Benny's chin. But Benny knows this trick. And keeps his mouth closed.

Of all of us you're the one we have to give the best food to. I'm looking after the girls as well, don't you doubt it, but we have to make sure that you get the best nutrients. Isn't that right. Isn't that right.

And the spoon curves higher in the air.

Isn't that right.

It swoops down and comes close to his mouth.

Ah ya, ah ya, that's right.

His father brings the lumped green to Benny's lips.

And we'll have you talking in no time. And all the wisdom of the world will come out of you.

The kitchen darkens suddenly: a cloud has eaten the sun. Benny reaches out his hands to grab it back.

You'll tell us everything, won't you, luveen.

But Benny keeps his mouth closed.

I still have a book of photos of the front doors of houses that I saw in a bookshop and told my father I wanted for my birthday. The cover was a mosaic of red

Georgian doors and butter-yellow half-doors and pointed studded Norman doors and dozens more. I thought of those doors as the last defence: keeping marauders out, keeping the secrets in. I used each of them to make up a story about the occupants. Later on I tried to get something about a door into each of my essays for honours English class. The teacher finally let me know that she'd noticed when I got an essay back with Yet another well-described door ... written in lettering like Snakes and Ladders up along the margin.

Now I can't even remember what the front door of his cottage had looked like before the fire.

When we moved to Newmarket-on-Fergus, we stayed there longer than any other place after Galway. The house was outside the town. One house next to it, then not much else. In fact when I think of those two houses they remind me of a pair of oak trees standing in the middle of a sea's worth of green field near Dromoland Castle. Remote but companionable. The door of our house was bright red. It gave a happy aspect to the house. On overcast days it held our shadows as we moved toward it. Shapes that looked a bit sinister; bruises on red fruit.

I loved that strawberry door.

I loved that house and the gravel crunching and settling under my feet and the fact that things in our life had finally seemed to settle too.

I loved how he had a story each evening from his job. Acorns, a wriggling nest of baby shrews. He measured between his fingers the size of a newborn shrew and I couldn't believe that something that size could make it in the forest at all. He drew his fingers in a point from Maeve's nose to show what the little shrew's snout was like.

I loved how he studied books to learn more about hedgerows and small animals. Books were calming to him and he set to them like a meal he'd been looking forward to all day.

Even when he revived the idea of living on an island, I loved the new, light lift in his voice, and I said that we almost were. Our neighbours were the neighbour island. Like Inisheer and Inishmaan, he said.

He wanted to keep us well and safe and healthy, he said. And so until I was twelve I must've eaten more brain food than most children. And now I wonder *if that wasn't part of my trouble as a teenager: I thought too much. I ran feelings and memories through my head like I was testing theorems.*

Did you ever hear that about fish being good for your brain?, *I say to the garda. He's sailing us slowly through a series of city traffic lights as if they're locks on a canal. We glide past a garden centre and shop windows and the lace-curtained front rooms of old red-brick houses. I've said this in a gabbly voice. Maybe because I haven't talked in a while, my voice came out wobbling like legs that have been sitting tightly crossed for hours. He takes it as nerves. And takes his hand off the wheel to pat mine. Instead of a there-there type of pat, it's solid and purposeful. When I blush I know it's because I'm not used to someone being so free with their kind feelings. I'm suddenly afraid I'm going to cry and that my voice will turn into the oily quack of trying to choke words back down.*

I did, I did alright, *he says.* Fish oils. The omega-threes are fierce fashionable these days.

Do you think you can eat your way to being happy, though? *At this, my garda could've given me the chary sidelong glance and looked at the clock to see how long he had left in this car with me.*

Instead he says, No. *Thoughtfully. Chewing on the idea for the taste of it.* No, I haven't. But there's probably some sense to it.

We ate fish and green vegetables. We ate so much brown rice that Maeve one time imagined she saw it coming alive on the plate, twisting and turning like a bed of maggots. Years later I saw a war film containing something like her terror, except it was a soldier remembering the nibbling of rats in a trench.

He told us that food had a tremendous effect on the workings of the brain. Serotonin. We can eat ourselves happy and healthy, *he'd announce in a ringmaster's voice.* We can make sure that we're not brought to despair.

That and all the exercise. I came to be glad that there was only one house next to us, and the people weren't outside very much. So they didn't see us jumping up and down like scissors. And our races up and down the long lawn. And the skipping. Ballerina, ballerina, turn around, ballerina, ballerina, touch the ground. *I had the harder time of it because Maeve on one end of the rope and our father on the other meant that the arc was all off, and I found myself veering toward him and the higher rope. His voice chanted the rhymes as zealously as girls in the schoolyard. I realized that I was afraid of how much I couldn't follow of his enthusiasms, his big plans to make us happy and healthy. We didn't feel all that different in spite of the chicken escalopes and all sorts of nuts and the sharp punching of our hearts after ten laps up and down the lawn.*

Lucky Benny was too small to be sent to aerobics. Instead he sat on the lawn on an anorak folded to a cushion and pulled on the grass with his dirty-dough hands. Sometimes he overbalanced. And that back lawn was where he learned to walk. We looked over to see him tipping off the anorak. Raising himself on his hands, face down, bottom high in the air. Then wide waddly steps. He looked like a saddle-sore cowboy arriving in town. Where can a man get a drink around these parts, pardner. Then the lawn came up to meet him and he sat down, spang-flat and starey, asking us with his sea-blue eyes if we'd seen what had just happened.

It was, I think, the first time I stopped being an older sister for a second and looked at him and saw what ladies in the supermarket saw. His beautiful quizzical face. The face that said, What? who, me? *When we were older and Maeve turned into the gorgeous one that everyone stared at hard and then turned away as if they'd been burned, she could well have used Benny's expression.* Me? *But Maeve never noticed her effect. And I never advertised it. Sisters don't give that kind of power to each other.*

Benny learned to walk and he never stopped surprising himself with the number of things he managed to crash into or pull down on top of himself.

He was nowhere as quick to talk. Sometimes I came upon our father trying to teach him. But it wasn't the same as teaching spelling or writing, where there's a formula. Our father seemed to think he could draw words from Benny like fruit that was whole and ready to be picked. Not the bleps *and* aks *and* fleeshes *that Benny favoured as his way to send noise into the world.*

I loved his funny wizardy words.

My brother nearly drowned because some one of us didn't notice him leaving the garage one time.

In one swift smooth curve the garda draws our car into a petrol station near the hospital.

We'll sit here for a few minutes and you can tell me about this. *He places his hand on mine again. This time it stays there, solid and warm and the hand I imagine him painting a door for his mother or cutting his father's hair when it starts to squirrel over his shirt collar.*

I tell him that Maeve is still sure it was her fault. And that she's had Benny glued to her side since he came out of the coma. And that she doesn't bother with boyfriends because they wouldn't understand that Benny has to go everywhere with her. In a way, she's the one still asleep, and walking through her life.

Benny's coma was short. We waited one day while he stayed under. Then he came back. At first it was though he'd gone on a long holiday and come back looking like himself. Then, as the days wound on, not himself at all. Never again. Something had been stolen on him. Our father used to wonder what Benny saw or heard that night on the beach; I just wanted to know what it was like to travel in his wintry sleep of that day.

I loved his still shape in the hospital bed. He was, I convinced myself, a time-traveller gone off to find amazing things in new worlds, other dimensions. He would come back with stories of fabulous cities and people who never got old and died. That's how I got through the silence and the stillness and the tubes and wires that branched from him like puppet strings.

I loved my sister and wanted to tell her that it would be alright and that she should stop crying because Benny could probably hear her and so she should start talking to him instead. She should tell him that the neighbour's cat had scratched her again and that we still had four of the doughnuts from the cake shop left to eat. Benny loved the jam that gouted from them. He eked out as much of it as he could and only then ate the pastry. The white sugar was his last pleasure, licked from fingers and the corners of his small mouth.

I wanted to know what Benny's sleep was like.

I wanted to be in it.

I didn't want him to ever tell our father what he had seen on the beach.

That was my job, really, and so I opened my mouth in the stinky-sweet hospital room, and told him that I'd seen our mother that night.

Daughters will always be a worry.

They joke about that in bars. Fathers get pitying looks from drinking companions. One time I listened to the father of four girls getting his whole life diagnosed for him. *Oh, sure, listen, you're never finished with daughters,* the man next to him pressing his wisdom the way some people coax a drink on you. Except he had no interest in buying a pint for the father of four. He was happier to pontificate. Like some fella marked from battle, but the stronger for it. *Never finished. First you've to watch them from the likes of predators as is going around these days. Then it's the schoolyard and fellas clobbering them. And soon enough you're onto discos and boyfriends.* I remember him widening his eyes at that part. As if he had seen the horrors. I imagined boyfriends with a whole hardware shop of chains hanging off them. Motorbikes. Drugs. I imagined thugs older than his daughters, men that squinted at him with weasel dark eyes. *By the time they've picked someone to marry you're only praying for some kind of a decent fella.* The silent, startled father of four daughters turned back to his pint and lapped it as if it held safety and good fortune in its rolling black depths.

Daughters would always be a worry. I knew this once I had two of them. And could imagine their growth into lovely girls and young women. When the English news had stories of missing girls, girls raped, girls butchered worse than animals, I felt like I was run through with a burning lance. I thought of those girls' fathers and how they must be driven out of their minds with fury. And how they, like me, would cut the throat of the bastard if they had a chance.

I know it seemed I had more love for my daughters than I had for my wife.

Belinda.

What would say if you could see our son this night here in this hospital?

What would you say about my terror at the sight of his still face? Cold as milk. Terror that I only knew once before: when they found you after your night in the sea. I sat with you then even though they wanted me to leave. Said it wasn't necessary; only identification was needed. But I asked for ten minutes. And stretched into it half an hour. You didn't look battered, like I was afraid of. You had only two big bruises. Where they were, on your jaw and temple, they looked like the marks left by sucking kisses. I remembered the time I left a mark on your neck like that. You were mortified that instead of dwindling it seemed to spread bigger each day. You wore scarves and high collars. But I saw you running your finger across it one time and the look on your face made me know that you were remembering the night of love that led to it.

Belinda.

When our boy came along I think you thought it was the thing I wanted most. And you had given it to me. And even if it meant that I would come to love Benny more than the girls, with you in third place, you had still borne this boy for me.

But Belinda, it was never like that.

I just loved the children differently. Like an animal protecting its nest of young.

Of course I should have made sure that you knew that you were loved too.

Instead I lingered back and let you get some happiness from Robin. I knew it from early on. Robin was always a transparent bollix. You, though. You were cagey. And I thought that silence and secrecy made the whole thing more appealing to you. I don't know how far it went with the two of you. And if Robin had left a mark on your neck would I have pretended not to see it. I just don't know. Whereas if one of the girls ever comes home with something like that I will probably tear down creation. But I just don't know.

You were always a bit of a closed book, of course. I put it down to being brought up in that house of brothers. At our wedding they surrounded you like bodyguards. All the things you must have had to keep to yourself in that house. And I think now about all the sadness you brought around with you from house to house. All our moves. I knew you were despairing of me. I knew it then and I never asked you straight out how you were feeling. We just stumbled on trying to fix this money problem or that one. Shoes for the children. Dinners to be made. You spun meals out of nothing sometimes, Belinda, and I was too fucking proud and shamed to acknowledge it.

Eva and Maeve have been taken back to your mother and father's for the night. It took Eva nearly half an hour to stop crying after she told me what she had to tell me. She would get hold of herself and go quiet and pale. And shudder until the crying started up again. I was thinking that a twelve-year-old should not have to cry like that. Nobody should, but least of all a young girl. Crying like a grown person who has known the saddest thing in the world.

She told me that she had seen you leave with Benny that night and that she didn't come to tell me. Even when she knew that there was something wrong about it. *I knew, Dadda, I knew that she shouldn't be going out in the dark with Benny.* It took her a long time, but she said that she thought you were going out to be with Robin. And that was why she didn't wake me. Eva. Suffering with this for so long.

There wasn't a way to ask her outright, but I wondered if she thought Benny was belonging to Robin. Of course we know he was ours. I clearly remember the night that we made him, for God's sake, and I don't know that there are many fathers who can say the same. It was funny, the way we both nodded at leaving the girls on the couch where they'd fallen asleep. And it wasn't like we had to sneak behind their backs in those days: they slept like nothing would wake them. Not a bomb or a flood or the sound of my heart banging on those times when I knew you wanted me. It wasn't all the time, of course. Things change, and they had changed between us. I put it down to having the girls and the way that becoming a mother had turned you into someone different. Not someone bad or cranky. You were just either busy or tired most of the time. And you thought you weren't nice to look at or love. After Maeve was born you carried extra weight for a long while. I didn't mind. I never minded. But you did. And you were happy when you thought it was finally going away. You were confident in yourself again.

There was something mischievous, sneaky even, about letting them sleep on downstairs. You led me to the bedroom. You drove things on like you never had before. It was an awful hard job not to spill all over you before I'd even gotten inside. You seemed like a stranger that night. No. Not a complete stranger. Like someone I'd seen in a bar or on a train and knew their face but nothing else. You kept saying that you needed it and needed it and needed it. We both felt it when I went deeper than any other time. They say you can't really tell that kind of thing, but you can. I kept going until I swore I was close to the place that had nested my daughters inside you. Belinda. I saw your smile shining like wet moonlight. You were never as beautiful as that night we made Benny.

And I don't know how to bring him back. I have failed you, Belinda. Even when you took him with you that night you never intended that he went all the way that you were going. You wrapped him up and hid him so carefully. Maybe it was the little bit of company you needed. Benny was always so warm and whispery when he was a baby. Maybe he was the last person you wanted to see. And any of the rest of us would have tried to stop you. I will never understand why you went into the sea, my Belinda. And I should have loved you more and harder and stronger to make sure that never happened.

Just like I should never have taken my eyes off Benny, not for one second, after that morning we found him under the rocks. God help me, but I tried not to. Women in the playground who rubbed their thumbs against his face. Children who ran helter-skelter around the buggy. I frightened them all off. I made them feel like kidnappers or just pure thugs. I am not proud of it. But I was doing my best. I was doing my best until he slipped out of the garage and went into the water.

And do you know why I was distracted, Belinda? Because I was reading some old magazine that reminded me of America. And I got to thinking about how I should have brought you over instead of me going back. I couldn't let go of the idea. The more I leafed through the pages of cornfields and the big green machinery you could buy to thresh it, the more my big mistake started to shout at me. *You fuckin' eejit, why didn't you make your life over there.* There would have been none of the scrabbling around for work like what happened once I came home. There would have been no in-laws to make us feel bad about our lot. I could have built a house for us for half-nothing. I looked across the garage at the girls and I thought they would have been happy in America. I should have stayed and Robin should have gone back. I could have made us an entirely different family. Still ourselves at heart, but different all the same.

Clean sunny America in that magazine distracted me and had me dreaming and killing myself over the bad choice I made. And that was when Benny made off. And I'm so sorry, Belinda, for everything.

I would do anything to feel your cool hand on the back of my neck. Telling me I am forgiven.

Cratloe and Bruff, 2001

House in the Woods

Small and made of lolly sticks, this house suits Benny down to the ground.

Down to the ground. He has collected these words from his grandfather, who said it when his grandmother took Benny by the shoulders and turned him round to show everyone his new coat. Benny slid his hands up and down the shiny blue sides, in and out of the big pockets. He did not know if he was supposed to stop turning and so he stayed spinning to show the coat to everyone in the kitchen: his grandfather, Eva, Maeve, and he wished that more and more people would come in to see this coat. Maeve laughed and told him that he could stop. When he didn't, she grabbed the end of the coat and pulled him to her. *You'll get a reel in your head and then you'll fall over and bang your head.* Then things on her face turned round, her eyes, her mouth, and then she let go of him, and then she was crying. Benny looked around for help. He didn't know what to do with her voice that flew up to the ceiling and hit the windows.

The anorak had soft woollen ends to its sleeves. He pulled his hands back inside them and used them to rub her face. He would do anything to make his sister stop crying. He knew this because there was a feeling in his stomach like being hungry for dinner. And when that feeling is there Benny will do anything to get rid of it.

Well wear. It suits you down to the ground. There are times when Benny doesn't remember that the man with the long narrow face and the red cheeks is someone he is supposed to know and be good to and quiet for when he is watching television. Sometimes he turns around and his grandfather is a stranger just arrived in the hall and Benny feels a scream punching out through his face. When his grandmother pulls the duvet high enough to tickle under his chin and rubs her hands down along his arms under the duvet, flattening him, making him still, he sometimes cries because of the strangeness of it. He looks and looks and then her face turns into one he knows: pink cheeks that he knows taste sweet and dry, like biscuits; eyes that sometimes seem to be looking at him through a rainy window. As long as he doesn't scream or cry then his grandfather and grandmother will always come back to him. If he screams and cries he frightens everyone and then himself because he sees all of their faces turned on him. Oh. Oh. Oh. All their mouths are round. All of their eyes look frozen like the eyes of the statues in the church.

He stays quiet in the church. He sits between his grandmother and Maeve. That's the best place for him. His grandmother always smells nice for church and Maeve is the one who minds him best. He doesn't like to be near the outside of the seat. It seems so high from the ground and he imagines slipping off the side and onto the hard floor. Maeve brings him to the top when she goes up to open her mouth for the white circle. He likes the lady statue, and he likes to go all the way to the top to be close to her. He knows that if he touches her she will be warmer than she looks. Her head is tilted to one side and her eyes look down. It's like she has dropped something at her feet and she's looking for it. It's like she might look up and ask him to pick it up for her someday.

He wears his new coat to church. He lets Maeve put a coin into the pocket so that he can take it out and drop it into the basket that goes past them. The sound of the basket is rattly and happy. The man that collects it at the end of the seat has big hands that look clumsy and red and might let the basket fall. He walks fast to the top, like he wants to drop the money and turn round and run all the way back to his seat. Benny would not like this job. Not if he had to go to the top all by himself. Benny sees that his face is red when he walks past.

One time there was a horrible smell that sneaked into Benny's nose when he wasn't paying attention. It came from something swung on the end of chains by the priest. It choked his eyes and throat. He started to cough and Maeve had to take him outside for fresh air. *Thanks, buster,* she said, kicking gravel in the yard. *I hate that stinky incense. I dunno how it doesn't poison the priest.* Benny knew that she was saying something she shouldn't be because her eyes lilted up to one side. She reminded him of a cartoon.

At the house in the woods there is a salty smell, but it's not a bad one. Benny doesn't know if it's the house itself or the woods leaking in. He likes the house down to the ground, right down to the shale path. Flat stones like black coins, dark-grey, orange-grey. He likes those ones best. They're a colour stones shouldn't be, and they leave a red trace on his hands. He uses them to scratch marks on the bigger darker stones. In the woods Benny finds a lot more to do than at his grandfather and grandmother's house. He can make his loudest sounds, make it seem like the whole world is full of shouting boys like him. His grandmother always looks frightened when he does that.

His father lets him scream to the tops of the trees.

His father walks with Eva and Maeve behind him. Benny runs. He likes how the path presses back against his feet, makes it harder to run.

In the woods everything takes more time.

When his father makes supper for them he does it in slower steps. First the fish fingers; he turns them over and over under a small square of flames. Then the saucepan of beans. After the beans he puts on a kettle that rocks and rattles as it boils to screaming. Benny loves the steps and pays attention to each one so that he can do this someday. He notices that the wet orange crust of the fish fingers turns brown-yellow and splits to show white beneath, and that's how he knows they are cooked. He sees that the bean sauce is redder after cooking than when it came tumbling out of the tin. His father moves knives and forks around on the table to make sure that everyone has enough elbow room. He folds squares of kitchen paper into triangles and sets them under glasses of milk. When the milk tastes bitter one evening, Benny waits for his sisters to stop drinking but they don't. Nobody says anything. Their father drinks water like he has always done, so he doesn't know about the bad taste reaching the back of Benny's mouth before he lets it slip down in one glug.

The bad-milk taste must be what the sea tastes like. More than the fish fingers, even though they have come from the sea. Benny often smells salt on the air, in many places. He's used to it prickling his nose.

When he sleeps next to his father in the house in the woods he doesn't know that the sea is on his face until his father rubs it away with his thumb. Benny wakes to this feeling. His father speaks to him. *Benny, oh my little lad, are you crying in your sleep, are you? Are you having a bad dream, are you?* His father lies back and circles Benny's wrist with his big dry hand. *I'll clip onto you like this and then you won't sail away from me.*

Benny could stay here forever, in the greenish darkness, with the smell of leaves and shale and wet twigs swirling around him. Those are his father's smell now, too. It feeds him and gives him games to dream about. Washing stones shaped like people's faces. Collecting leaves, lifting them to see things squiggling in the dirt. Hiding his findings in a drawer at his grandparents' house, lining them up on the floor. Delving his hands into bits of his father and the woods.

Maeve's grandmother says that their house is in a dell and she should never have been convinced to marry and move to *this accursed corner of the country*. She runs down Bruff quite often, and Maeve used to find it strange that a woman of her age would be as vexed at the place as Maeve and Eva were. Boring Bruff. A house sunk in a hollow.

But when her grandmother makes these complaints it's always when their grandfather is around. She wants him to hear because she doesn't really mean it all that much. It's a joke between them, one to which he says nothing at all. But Maeve can tell by the way he winks at her and Eva that he likes when their grandmother play-acts like this. Maeve is beginning to realize that grown-ups, even very old ones, have their special ways of mocking each other.

Sometimes it's like the way boys in her school grab the back of her coat, pull hard, and then vanish when she turns around. Something is meant by this. The other girls tell her that boys do it to get her attention, that those boys like her. But this gives Maeve a tight feeling in her stomach: she doesn't want to have to dread going to school because some boy might leave a note in her coat pocket. She doesn't want the feeling that she has to do something back, or else be mean to him. She knows she could never be like her grandmother, with her high voice and her mouth pursed after she's made a jibe about the house and its dampness.

The previous winter, when the rain was heavy for days and days, their grandmother was sure that it was going to flood. Especially the kitchen. The grassy hill leading down to the back yard was steep, a high green wall. Maeve's grandmother blocked the back door with rolled-up sacks. *If enough rain falls,* she said, huffing as she stuffed the sack, *it'll run down that hill and on in here and the next thing you know we'll have saucepans and shoes sailing around the place.* Yet she seemed amused thinking about this. She chucked Benny under the chin and told him that he might have to get a little boat to row them around. The way he looked at her made Maeve want to laugh. Are you cracked or something, his disapproving eyes said.

This was around the time that all Benny did was stare at things. After they moved to Bruff he spent almost a year taking things in through his wide eyes. He ate up television and visitors to the house. He gazed into the bath water as if there was something down there that only he could see. They all knew that he was never going to be the same after what happened to him in the barrel. They had their own ways of being around this different Benny. At first Maeve was afraid of him. When Eva let go of his hand and propelled him to Maeve to play with, she felt herself stepping back. I don't want to, I don't want to, she heard inside her head. When he came to her there was a smell of whatever he'd spilled on his clothes at the table. Milk. Soup. Other times he smelled of the toilet and she was sure that he'd splashed himself instead of getting it all inside the rim. His hands were often grimy; dark lines criss-crossed his palms. The kind of ground-in dirt that you could turn into little black ants if you rubbed your hands hard together.

For a while she was ashamed of her dirty, smelly, little brother. Angry that he had to be brought to the sink to wash himself. She hated the feeling of squelching the soap suds in and out through his fingers, using a hair clip to wiggle dirt from under his nails. She hated how still he stood when she cleaned, or when she changed him out of wet trousers or dragged socks off his feet. He was her statue brother and she couldn't love him any more.

But she knew it was more her job, and Eva's, much more than their grandparents'. They had all the patience in the world for Benny, and Maeve didn't know where hers had disappeared to. Eva hauled him here and there like a puppy and didn't seem to be put out by him at all. Sometimes she shouted at him as if he were older, like a boy in her class. *Ah, for God's sake Benny, would you mind what you're doing and not be spilling Rice Krispies all over the shop.* All over the shop. Would you get to hell. Eva picked up some new expressions from secondary school. When she used them on Benny sometimes it sounded to Maeve like the way their grandparents spoke to each other. Annoyance. Words that smacked hard because someone or other was being a nuisance. The time their grandfather left a Mass leaflet in his pocket and it came apart in the washing machine and shed paper flakes all over the clothes. The time their grandmother put on a kettle without water and a small fire started inside its white walls. The time Benny opened a biro and spread ink all over Eva's essay. *Benny, you feckin' little bastard.* And then she started laughing. And then Benny laughed too. It was the first time in Maeve didn't know how long that he had made a sound. His laugh ribboned out around the kitchen, up and down and on and on. Maeve thought she might cry with jealousy that Eva was the one who brought his voice back.

But when Maeve helped him to wash that night she got him back to her, too. She leaned in and smelled his face before she brought the hot cloth to it. Like stewing meat. And all of a sudden she remembered when he was a baby and used to paint his face with whatever was mashed for him to eat. This was Benny's face from years ago. And he was still a baby. She folded him into her. At first his arms were captured by his sides. Then he wiggled them free and put them around her neck. They stayed like that in the bathroom until Eva came banging to use it. *She's forever taking baths,* isn't she, Maeve whispered into Benny's hair.

When the time comes that they can all visit their father, Maeve watches him take Benny to him like she had done. A hug so tight it could maybe kill him. Their father presses kisses down on Benny's head and half-carries him into the wooden house. Maeve and Eva follow a few steps behind. It's as if they are afraid of what the inside will be. When they cross the threshold they see that their father has already put Benny sitting at a square table covered with red-checked oilcloth. Maeve takes the room in: it's both a kitchen and a living room. A door to the back must be his bedroom. A low couch, covered with a blanket. It's a car seat. She can see the metal coils and foam under the blanket that doesn't meet the ground. It looks like a place that kids have turned into a house. No television. Books stacked to the height of Benny all along one wall. The place unsettles her with its clutter; it makes her think of the garage full of the old man's things that they half-cleaned out. And when she thinks of that day she wants to run back out to the air. Not much light is coming in. The air is a thickened grey. Their father flicks a switch and a bulb comes to life over the table. It hangs lower than bulbs usually do. It makes Benny look like a person in the detective programmes that her grandmother loves, somebody about to get asked lots of questions about a murder.

When Benny gives one of his yelps the awkward feeling snaps. Maeve has never been so grateful for her brother's strange moody noises. Sometimes they vex her when they're out in a supermarket and he wants her attention on a brick of ice-cream or a baby in a buggy, but now she likes his chirpy demand that something happen here in this house. Their father asks if they'd like some tea and biscuits. Benny eats Toffypop after Toffypop.

Because this is the first visit they won't be staying long. He tries to make things like they used to be, by giving them a lesson on this place. *The Cratloe Woods,* he says, *used to be oak trees that went back thousands of years. You'd have read about that time in your history book in school. Back when Ireland was nearly carpeted in forest.* His job is to tend to the trees. Mind the newly planted ones and check for any kind of interference by animals or parasites. *They say that Cratloe oak beams went over to London for the roof of Westminster Hall.*

The same stuff that he used to talk about: history and land and trees and creatures. But his voice and his way of looking at them has changed. When he used to give his lessons he would look at each of them, turn by turn, holding them with his eyes. It made Maeve remember things, this serious stare he distributed with his words. It was how she would always be responsible for knowing the names of four of the men executed after the 1916 Rising. She got Clarke, MacDonagh, Ceannt and Plunkett; Eva got MacDiarmada, Pearse and Connolly. But this time his eyes wander above their heads when he talks. Like he's addressing some people standing behind them, and Maeve feels her neck prickle at the thought.

Because he isn't holding their eyes it means that she can examine him closely. She hasn't seen him for almost a year, and that was on her birthday. They met him in Limerick city and they had chicken and chips for lunch. He asked the restaurant if they would put candles on a cake he'd brought. He was dressed up in a shirt and tie, and he had a book called *Ghosts, Ghouls and Goblins* for her. There was a round sticky grey patch where he'd taken the price tag off. She pressed her fingers to its glueyness any time she held the book to read it. Eventually it annoyed her and she scraped it off with the blade of a scissors. Under the lemony light from the bulb she sees that his neck has some small beads of dried blood from shaving. His hair is a bit long around his ears; it flicks up in dark wings and she wants to smooth them down. His eyes. The skin under them is worn. It's like he's been tugging it down with his thumbs. Then she remembers the story of Saint Peter. The teacher reading: *He wept with such regret that the tears coursed down and wore tracks down along his face.* She loved how that sounded. When he walks them back through the woods and out to a parking place, their grandfather's car is running and he has the radio on loud enough for them to hear it at a distance. One of the hurling or football matches. The commentator is shrill and excited. *And the man from Milltown is away with the ball.* Maeve thinks his high, almost tearful voice sounds daft pouring off into the trees where nobody will hear it, but still she's glad of it. A silent car would mean that their grandfather was uneasy while he waited. Their father takes Benny's hands and gives one each to Maeve and Eva. He stops at the saplings that hem the woods. And backs into them, like a magician vanishing behind a stage curtain.

Maeve would see him more often after that. She would go with Eva and Benny, sometimes just with Benny, and other times Eva would go by herself.

Their grandfather would drop them at the lay-by near the saplings that were growing taller and stouter, like boys when they came back to school after the summer.

Each visit would be easier than the last. Because she knew that her father was different, for good and ever. And once that settled in her heart, she knew that she would be able to love him, in spite of his faraway eyes and the slow trouble he took with making sandwiches and the fact that there were no photos of them, or their mother, anywhere in the small wooden house in the woods.

I got my own bedroom in Bruff. The house was old and the rooms big. But always chilly, even in summer. Our grandmother brought out the heavy eiderdowns when winter really set in and turned the bedrooms into cold compartments that it was dicey to walk in without your socks. My eiderdown was dark-pink and ruffed all the way around. She'd made all of them when she was a young woman and new to the house. I couldn't imagine how she'd hefted the weight of it around her in order to appliqué the big pink rose in the middle. I liked the eiderdown because it kept me from kicking around in bed, looking for that comfortable sleeping place. It held me still under its heaviness and helped me fall asleep quicker. Maybe like babies are supposed to be calmed and comforted by wrapping them tightly.

I thought this made such sense that one day I folded Benny into the pink eiderdown and kept turning him inside it until he was fully wrapped. I fastened it with one of our grandfather's belts. I did it because he was losing it. He did this in the days after getting his voice back. Shrieking what our grandmother called *blue murder*. But she was furious when she saw him rolled up on the living-room carpet, eyes fixed on the ceiling, feet pointing out to left and right. *What in the name of God did you do? Do you want Benny to be taken away from us?*

That was back at the time when we had visits from nurses and social services, making sure that our grandparents were able to look after our damaged brother. But maybe it was Maeve and me they should've been weighing up, too. Just because we were his sisters didn't mean that we didn't get cross with him. Often. Maeve just showed it more. I kept my feelings held somewhere else, away from words and actions that other people could see. One day when Benny spilled hot soup on my hand I stared at him so hard that it felt like all the heat was leaving my burned skin and pouring out through my eyes. And he caught it. And he looked back until we were both frightened by me and my hardness and my want to make him behave like the brother he would've been without the accident.

After that I softened. My shame turned me into his best friend for a while. I let him away with things. I helped him finish a full bag of mini-Mars bars. I said to a woman in the supermarket, *Something to look at?* when I saw her gazing at Benny with saintly sympathy. Bitch, I thought to myself, at least my brother wasn't born retarded like your kids probably were.

I was very tough around that time. *A right tough nail*, as our father used to say about certain fathers of children at our schools. Children who always looked hungry and wary.

The only thing that stopped me being a monster to my grandparents was their age. It just didn't seem possible, not with the see-through skin on their hands and their wavery eyes. They might break into little pieces. Saying the nasty things I felt would've been like mugging them.

I started to ease up when we began to see our father again.

For the first visit all three of us go together.

I watch him pick up Benny in a way that reminds me of the day he pulled him from the barrel. I stop breathing at the sight of it. I watch him lift Benny outside the wooden house and hold him tightly and sway him side to side in a heavy hug.

For the first time, I think that the day my brother came out of the water was worse than the morning after the storm when our mother was lost. Our father moaning and crying. Lowering the barrel to the ground. Water filling the yard and pooling blackly around our shoes, Benny's feet hanging out of the rim. Benny in our father's arms, water raining from his clothes and hair, turning our father's clothes black. Benny's white wet face and slicked-darker hair. Eyes closed, lips shut tight. I remember his arms dangling longer than they should've been. But then I saw that his sleeves were longer because water makes wool heavy.

Maeve and I watched our father press his mouth on Benny's. Covering his lips like a kiss between lovers. It shocked me more than the hungry whanging of the emptied barrel rolling side to side.

One time I'd seen our father and mother locked together like this. Just once. Above Benny's buggy. They didn't know I saw it. It was outside a burger place; they thought Maeve and I were still inside trying to get the metal claw machine to pick up a teddy-bear. I left Maeve to have the last go. I saw them through the window. My mother stepped out of the kiss first; she backed away as if it had begun to burn her. I didn't know what to make of it, and turned back to see Maeve jumping up and down and begging the claw to deliver the bear all the way to her. And it did. By the time we were back in the car I'd forgotten the kiss and how it had looked like messy eating.

After kissing Benny there was telephoning and an ambulance and the hospital.

And after that there was a different Benny and our father gave us to our grandparents to be looked after because he didn't think he had done a proper job of it.

Not seeing him for a long time was as much about our disappointment as his shame. He was the one who'd come up with the idea of going to live by himself. The let-down made Maeve and not want to see him full stop. We sort of knew where he lived, and it was in the same county, but for a year it might as well have been somewhere at the bottom of the world. Tasmania. I looked at it on a map in school and thought, that's his kind of place. But time passed and we softened. We had to. A father is a father, and ours hadn't done anything truly bad. He wasn't one of the tough-nail fathers.

The first visit shocks me because of the hug. And because of the awful sad smell of his bathroom: shaving cream and what was under the rim of the stained toilet. The books with buckled covers. The car seat that made Maeve look like a long-legged cowboy when she flumped down onto it.

I go on my own for the second visit. I ask our grandmother if there might be an extra eiderdown and if I could take it. I can see that she wants to say, *No there isn't*. But if there's one thing she hates it's a lie, and she has to tell me that *Yes, there's an extra one*. In which case she has to let me bring it. I thought of our grandmother when I came across the word *alms* in Religion class. She'd do things like that just so she could think of herself as a good alms-giving lady. There wasn't any badness in that, I thought; it meant that people were getting the stuff they needed. I bale a blue eiderdown and force it into a big black bin bag. It feels funny carrying it from the car to the stile that we climb over to get to the woods. He is there waiting. And for the first time in ages he laughs. At me, wobbling under the bag.

And I get my first period during that visit. For a week I'd had a clawing feeling in my belly. Being dragged down, down, something rummaging round to turn me inside out. We're at the table playing twenty-five when I soak. I back into the bathroom and think I'm going to be sick at the sight. Brown-red has filled my pants and come out through my trousers. It looks as wet and shiny as jam. I know what it is, but still it feels like the end of the world. I want to sit on the toilet forever. He comes knocking after a long time has passed. I start crying, and he knows what's happened. *Now, we won't panic. There's no need to panic. We'll figure this out, love.* His voice is in charge. I love the sound of it, because it doesn't hesitate and it knows how to help me. *You'll need to give me a few minutes, alright.* So I sit there, getting colder. More blood flourishes down into the toilet; I look between my legs and see it join the water and spread like red clouds. Then I hear a knock and before I can stand up my father is in the bathroom. His back is turned to me. He stretches his arm behind him and gives me a pale blue wad. I see that it's the cotton of a shirt, cut neatly and folded lots of times. *This'll have to do until you get back.*

Sitting on it feels strange, but somehow we manage to pass another hour. We have tea and custard cream biscuits. I feel my stomach relaxing. He tells me that he's been reading a lot about oil rigs. *It seems like a sensible kind of a job. There for a couple of months on end, and then back onto land where your time is your own until it's time to go back.* He looks me full in the eyes. *It'd be the kind of place where a fella could come back to himself.* I think, Tasmania. This is my fault because I wanted him gone to some far-flung place in the sea.

When I start crying he thinks it's because of the period. *Now, love, your grandmother mightn't tell you this, but your own mother suffered from tears around her time of the month.* I cry more because he has mentioned her. At long last. And because his hand rubs my back firmly. Maybe he soothed her like this when she had hers. Now I'm sobbing because I think of them and how they must've been happy sometimes. Looking after each other. Jabbing each other with funny spiky words like our grandparents. By the time he takes me along the path to the car I've forgotten the seriousness in his voice when he talked about the oil rig.

After that I would meet him with Maeve and Benny sometimes, a few more times by myself. When I got older we would see each other for lunch in town; we would shop for trousers and shoes for him. Go to the library for books for both of us.

And I would come to find excuses for meeting him in more and more places other than the cabin.

He would try to teach me to drive.

Build a big shed at the back and keep hens. Bernie and Doris and Mary-Angela: middle-aged ladies' names. *Eggs with pure golden hearts*, he'd say. Eventually they would exasperate him and he'd complain about them in fond grumbles, the way hens themselves seemed to give out as they tutted about the place.

He would get a little odder with each year by himself, expecting the world to end in a nuclear holocaust or just being afraid of getting murdered in his home. When this change set in I would take charge of meeting him more than Maeve and Benny.

It would be my job from now on.

Handling our father.

Our father besieged by the world's nightmares, big and small. Our father who I imagined dreamed most nights of dark water and the ones he loved in it. If he shouted in his sleep only the whispering trees would hear it. And shiver among themselves at the loneliness of the man in their midst.

After I've talked to them inside the station maybe I'll tell this garda that Benny sometimes wears a pearl necklace and nobody looks too hard at it because they already see that something's different about my brother. It sits inside his shirt collar. A row of round baby teeth that he touches every so often.

That for a long time my sister Maeve has wanted us to ring Robin and see how he is, but I've always said no. And that now might be the time to do it. I tried to put him out of mind because of all our times that he stood for. We have the address and phone number of every place he's lived, Belfast, Manchester, Melbourne, written inside Christmas cards that got a bit smaller and cheaper each year. Their soft paper and lone burning candles reminded me of everything I imagined about Robin's life since he left us.

We've parked at the end of a fleet of white cars. Two gardaí get out of the car next to us; one of them opens the back door and a boy of about fourteen gets out. His head is lowered. Shame or fear, or maybe so much anger that if he looks up he will try to strike one of these men, and so he keeps his eyes mooched on the ground. I can't imagine what he's done, but I feel bad for him because he has ferocious acne flaring up along his neck and jaws. I used to think it was desperately wrong that teenagers were persecuted with skin that bad. It seemed like something they should get much later on in life, a kind of payback for drinking and smoking and eating badly.

I remember seeing a photo of my father taken when he was in his late teens and his cheeks were colonized by spots. He looked self-conscious. Caught out by the camera. Because it was a Polaroid his skin was white as a hard-boiled egg and the spots stood out, distinctly dotted like measles.

I watch the boy walk between the two gardaí and I see that he is cuffed. His runners are big and crumpled at the tops, his tracksuit bottoms have button fasteners all down the sides. Maybe we, Maeve and I, are lucky that Benny stopped growing up when he did. That he never got in with boys and their tribes and the trouble they cause.

I tell my garda to go in ahead of me and that I'll meet him in the front hall. I raise the diary: one last part to read. When he says, Of course, you're grand, come in when you're ready and I'll be at the front desk, *I think that this might be the kind of fella to make an effort with. The kind who would take me and Maeve and Benny in his stride and build safety around us. Because the fact is, any fella I consider will have to consider my sister and brother too.*

He closes the car door softly and I'm left with the final few pages.

21 October 2006

You have to know when to hold 'em, know when to fold 'em.

The fact that I remember the song Robin sang every day for a fortnight when we were painting a house in Cape Cod means something today. Robin up at the top of a ladder singing this damnable song every single day. As if he was trying to perfect it. It nearly drove me demented. But I would be happy to hear him hammering away at it now. When he walked out of the house in Barna that day we both knew that was that. Over and done with. Shameful carry-on, when we could have both been of some help to each other as time went on. I know what it has been like to grieve for Belinda. I should have considered that it might have been something like that for him. I should have thought about that. Men can be the worst of proud eejits. Can never let their guard down. Never give an inch. Nothing through the chinks. Robin and myself could have sat together across a table or at a bar and let the question thicken and settle between us. Why she did it. We would never have come up with an answer, but knowing that the other person was thinking about it too, well that would have been a useful thing. Worriting about the same awful thing. I liked the word when I came across it in a book of children's poetry bought for the girls. *He worrited in the dead dark of every night.*

My children come to visit but they are slipping loose of me. I am not able to look after them any more. And I think maybe I never was. With children you have so much love that you can be sensible with it or you can let it paralyse you. You can parcel it out in laughing and hi-jinks and still make sure that they are getting the practical things from you too. Or you can spend years making the love perfect and pure, working on it like a sculpture. And in the end it is dead cold and cannot twist or turn.

I have been thinking about the best way out of this. I have been thinking about what I could do to make myself better. There are places a man can go to work where he will work so hard that all the worry gets burned out of him. Mining. Drilling. The merchant navy. I have looked into these things. I have examined what place in the world might offer a man like me berth for a time. I have come to like photographs of oil rigs. Steel islands. Some of them standing like big black crane-flies in the sea. Others like yellow cities on stout legs. Fixed platforms, jack-up plat-forms, spar platforms. You can be on a rig so far out as not to see the shore at all. The Gulf of Mexico and its hur-ricanes. The North Sea. Texas and Azerbaijan. What I like most about all the information in the book is that crews work long, long shifts. I can see myself doing this. I can imagine listening to the groaning of the rig at midnight and thinking I was the only person left in the world.

I will clean out my head and my heart this way. In the middle of the sea. This is what I will do, and I will do it for as long as it takes. I am looking around this cabin now and thinking how much I hate its walls and floors and shabbiness and smell. I won't even leave it behind me when I go. At last I think I know when to fold things.

I don't know why I turn the page expecting something more from him. But looking at its emptiness, marked only by the heavily dug words on the page before, I realize that he wouldn't have thought to leave something specifically addressed to us. He wrapped up his secrets and sadness in the diary and left it where the fire wouldn't swallow it. The whole thing is meant for us. All its words are true.

Even though it might take years, he will be back from where he went.

So when I meet my garda in the front hall I will follow him to whoever I need to speak with. I will listen. I will be polite. I will answer questions. And I will tell them that I do not want him found. Located would be their word. As though the person gone missing is a feature on a map.

And I will find some way to hold onto the diary.

I will sit with Maeve and Benny and look through pictures of oil rigs. On every one of them we will imagine him. Sleeping in a bunk bed. Singing his country songs as he works. Rhinestone Cowboy and Streets of Laredo. Studying the sea's sounds and moods and colours, saving up its thousand details for us.

And when he tells us about wild weather and whales, and draws the shapes of machinery with his hands, and mimics the voices of other workers, he will be older and hardier and more knowledgeable than ever. His voice will be brimming gladness to be back. Maeve and Benny and I will fold ourselves around him like I once saw children in a film do. They were beggars who accosted a tall man with a kind face. He bent over to tie his shoelace and they poured down on him and beseeched him to take them home.

Acknowledgments

I am most grateful to Faith O'Grady. First reader, best reader, and true to her name.

In earlier work I have been fortunate to work with several fine editors. I thank in particular Bill Pierce for his attentive readings, mentorship and devilment. I also thank Peter Campion, Sven Birkerts, Colum McCann, Jennifer Barber, Peter Brown and Declan Meade.

Thanks too to Fiona Dunne for the pleasure of working with her on the fine-tuning of these pages, and to Gordon Lish for a lovely correspondence about sentences.

Though they were not directly involved in this novel, I am grateful for the generous support of Massachusetts Cultural Council and the Babson College Faculty Research Fund in other fiction-writing endeavours.

My Arts and Humanities colleagues are the cheeriest and most supportive that anyone could wish for.

The Boston Athenæum was my home for the writing of this book, and I am lucky to enjoy the sustaining friendship of Monica Higgins, Carolle Morini and Melissa Allen.

Certain people – friends, writers and scholars – deserve my warmest thanks for their generosity, encouragement, and thoughtful readings. Among them I count *cara* Lisa Colletta, Miguel Rivera, Louis de Paor, John Connolly, Mary Pinard, Sue Miller, Jon Dietrick, Ronan Noone, Craig Robertson and Aidan Rooney.